W9-AAK-742

REUNITED...

"You must be Matt. I'm Greg Mazlin. And this is my daughter." He reached behind him and literally yanked the reluctant girl into the kitchen. "Matt, meet Dina."

The next few seconds extended forever. Dina and I stared at each other. Her mouth dropped open. I could feel my face grow red and hot.

Suddenly my mom shrieked in excitement. "Greg, come over here! It's that pair of cardinals I was telling you about." Mr. Mazlin rushed over to my mom's side. Dina and I just stood there.

As I stared at her familiar, precious face a hundred flashbacks competed with one another in my mind: Dina skiing sleekly down the mountain, her shoulder-length blond hair streaming behind her. Dina at the opposite end of the couch in front of the lodge fire, writing in her diary as I rubbed her feet after a long day on the slopes. Dina giggling on the chairlift at some stupid joke I had cracked, her blue eyes sparkling. I tried to speak, but no words came out of my mouth. Should I announce that we had already met? Should I say what I was really feeling? Or would "I love you" sound too strong?

Before I had realized it, the moment had passed. Dina reached out her hand.

"Nice to meet you, Matt." She looked calm, but her hand was shaking as I took it in mine.

Don't miss any of the books in *Love Stories*
—the romantic series from Bantam Books!

#1 *My First Love* . . . . Callie West

#2 *Sharing Sam* . . . . Katherine Applegate

#3 *How to Kiss a Guy* . . . . Elizabeth Bernard

#4 *The Boy Next Door* . . . . Janet Quin-Harkin

#5 *The Day I Met Him* . . . . Catherine Clark

#6 *Love Changes Everything* . . . . ArLynn Presser

#7 *More Than a Friend* . . . . Elizabeth Winfrey

#8 *The Language of Love* . . . . Kate Emburg

#9 *My So-called Boyfriend* . . . . . . Elizabeth Winfrey

#10 *It Had to Be You* . . . . Stephanie Doyon

#11 *Some Girls Do* . . . . Dahlia Kosinski

#12 *Hot Summer Nights* . . . . Elizabeth Chandler

#13 *Who Do You Love?* . . . . Janet Quin-Harkin

#14 *Three-Guy Weekend* . . . . Alexis Page

#15 *Never Tell Ben* . . . . .Diane Namm

#16 *Together Forever* . . . . .Cameron Dokey

#17 *Up All Night* . . . . .Karen Michaels

#18 *24/7* . . . . Amy S. Wilensky

SUPER EDITIONS

Listen to My Heart . . . . Katherine Applegate

Kissing Caroline . . . . Cheryl Zach

It's Different for Guys . . . . .Stephanie Leighton

Coming soon:

#19 *It's a Prom Thing* . . . . Diane Schwemm

24/7

Amy S. Wilensky

BANTAM BOOKS
NEW YORK · TORONTO · LONDON · SYDNEY · AUCKLAND

To the biggest pest I know.
Love always, and carpe diem.

RL 6, age 12 and up

24/7
A Bantam Book / May 1997

Produced by Daniel Weiss Associates, Inc.
33 West 17th Street
New York, NY 10011.
Cover photography by Michael Segal.

All rights reserved.
Copyright © 1997 by Daniel Weiss Associates, Inc., and
Amy S. Wilensky.
Cover art copyright © 1997 by Daniel Weiss Associates, Inc.

No part of this book may be reproduced or transmitted
in any form or by any means, electronic or mechanical,
including photocopying, recording, or by any information
storage and retrieval system, without permission in
writing from the publisher.
For information address: Bantam Books.

If you purchased this book without a cover you should be aware
that this book is stolen property. It was reported as "unsold and
destroyed" to the publisher and neither the author nor the pub-
lisher has received any payment for this "stripped book."

ISBN: 0-553-57074-9

Published simultaneously in the United States and Canada

Bantam Books are published by Bantam Books, a division of Bantam
Doubleday Dell Publishing Group, Inc. Its trademark, consisting of the
words "Bantam Books" and the portrayal of a rooster, is Registered in
U.S. Patent and Trademark Office and in other countries. Marca
Registrada. Bantam Books, 1540 Broadway, New York, New York 10036.

PRINTED IN THE UNITED STATES OF AMERICA

OPM   0 9 8 7 6 5 4 3 2 1

PROLOGUE

"I LOVE YOU, Dina."

Matt's voice was so quiet that I barely heard the words. His arms tightened around me. It had just started to snow. Thick white flakes landed in his hair and glistened like diamonds. Although the temperature was dropping toward zero, I wasn't cold. My face felt warm, and hot tears moistened my cheeks. I had taken off my gloves so that I could feel Matt's hands in mine, but even my fingers were warm.

"I love you too," I whispered. I gazed into his eyes, wishing this moment would never end.

I had never felt like this before. I had never even imagined I *could* feel this way.

"Hey, lovebirds. Get out of the chairlift line!" Two guys skied past us, bumping into me as they rushed to get on the lift for one last run down the mountain.

"Relax!" I yelled to them, brushing the snow off my ski pants. So much for our perfect moment.

"We were standing right in their path," Matt pointed out to me.

He held out his hand. Once again I clasped his fingers with mine. We walked slowly to the front door of the lodge where we had spent so many blissful hours learning everything there was to know about each other.

At the door Matt leaned forward and brushed his lips softly against my forehead. More tears streamed down my face. He kissed them away as I tried to regain my composure.

"You promised," Matt reminded me. "No crying." His eyes were bright as he held me lightly around the waist. "No crying, no regrets."

I nodded. "I know. I'm sorry." And I was.

I had told myself a hundred times not to do this. Not to make leaving Matt one of the saddest moments of my life. We had agreed that we wanted to remember each other happy, the way we had been since the moment we'd met a week before. Matt had said if we were meant to be together, we'd find each other again someday. But good-bye was good-bye. And it was wrenching.

Matt pulled me close and kissed my tear-streaked cheek one last time.

I sighed deeply. "I just wish . . ."

"What?" Matt asked. His voice trembled. "What do you wish?"

I swallowed hard and shook my head. "Nothing."

There was no point in making this moment harder for both of us. Matt had to go back to California, and I had school tomorrow. In Boston. Our time together had come to an end, and there was absolutely nothing that either of us could do about it.

For the millionth time I realized that life was hard. And unfair. It seemed that I always had to say good-bye to the people I loved.

"It's getting late," Matt whispered after a few moments.

The sun was setting, and the sky was turning the indigo blue of night. Skiers bustled around us, heading into the lodge after a long day on the slopes.

I looked at my watch. 4:00 P.M. Oops. Dad had told me to be back in our rooms by four o'clock on the dot. I was already late. Our flight to Logan International Airport left in exactly two hours.

"No good-byes, right?" I tried to smile.

Matt squeezed my hand. He swallowed hard. "Right. No good-byes."

He held my fingers for a moment longer. Then he let go of my hand and turned toward the lodge. A second later he had disappeared through the double swinging doors. And I was alone.

For almost a minute I stood frozen. My feet felt glued to the snow-covered ground. Then a woman in a hot pink ski suit tapped me on the arm.

"Are you okay?" she asked. She was looking at me as if I had grown a third eye or something.

I forced myself to smile. "I'm fine," I assured her. *At least I hope I'll be fine. Someday.*

I turned and walked into the lodge. My boring, regular life was waiting for me in Boston. And my dad was probably pacing back and forth, waiting for me in his hotel room.

Life went on. If I had learned anything in my almost seventeen years, it was that—no matter what, life went on.

3/21

Dear Diary,

It's me again. Bet you thought I'd disappeared for good. I don't think I've gone so long without writing since I had mono freshman year. Anyway, I'm sitting here on the plane, on the way back from the most incredible week of my life. And I just haven't had time for you. Okay, that's not exactly true. It's just that I've been in another world. Well, not exactly another world; more like another planet. If you can call Mount Blizzard in northern Colorado another planet. As usual I'm rambling without ever getting to the point. I'll just tell you what happened. . . .

As you know, my dad and I had planned a ski trip with his college roommate Elliott and Elliott's daughter, who's also sixteen. But of course with my luck, as soon as I get there I find out that Ellen—Elliott's daughter—has sprained her ankle and isn't coming after all. So at first I thought, *Oh, great. I get to spend the week all alone while my dad makes up for lost time with Elliott.*

And I did spend the first day of vacation skiing all by myself. Dad and Elliott offered to let me tag along with them. But listening to stories about frat parties and football games that took place over twenty years ago isn't my idea of a good time. Anyway, after a whole day of listening to nothing but the sound of wind in my ears, I decided I needed to find some company. So the next morning I signed up for a snowboarding class.

Lucky for me, I was the only person who felt snowboarding was a worthwhile activity. Because it turned out the whole class consisted of me . . . and The Instructor. Let me tell you, he was the most gorgeous guy I had ever laid eyes on.

At first I was speechless. Who could talk when faced with that toothpaste-commercial smile? But finally I managed to say that he could just give me my money back if he didn't want to teach a class for one. He just smiled, said his name was Matt, and promised to give me a snowboarding lesson I'd never forget.

For the rest of the week we were together every possible minute. Dad was so busy with Elliott that he didn't even bother me about meeting Matt. Thank goodness. Dads aren't the greatest catalyst for romance.

So Matt and I spent our days on the slopes, except when he had to teach classes. At night we hung out at the lodge in front of the fire.

Unfortunately Matt goes to school in California (he was just teaching classes during spring break to earn some extra cash). And I've lived in the same Boston suburb for my entire life.

We didn't let ourselves talk about the future—and the fact that we'd probably never see each other again. But we did talk about real things, important things. Things I can't even talk about with Alison, my best friend in the whole world. For instance, he's the first person I was ever really able to talk to about my mom. You know, stuff like how it feels to miss her every single day and how fragile and quiet she was in the hours before she died. And he told me about his parents' divorce and how much he wanted them to get back together. He said it was the most important thing in his life for them to be a family again. And get this: He keeps a diary too! Only he calls it a journal. I guess that sounds more masculine. . . .

The best moment by far, though, was at the very top of Mount Blizzard on the afternoon we'd decided to try the black diamond slope, the last day of spring break. We stood side by side, gazing down the mountain, trying to pick the best route. Suddenly I felt a certain tension in the air. When I looked at Matt, he was looking at me, deep into my eyes. Without saying a word we leaned closer to each other, then closer . . . and then we were kissing.

I had never been kissed like that before, and I doubt I ever will be again. The black diamond slope seemed tame after that kiss—let's put it that way.

I'll never forget Matt . . . not for as long as I live.

ONE

DINA

"WELL, TO BE totally honest, Dad, the place looks pretty bad to me." I took a huge step back from the curb to get a wider view of the damage.

Thanks to Hurricane Pam, our formerly charming brick apartment building was no longer quite so charming. What a way to start the summer! It was only the middle of June, but already I felt as though my summer were over.

My dad sighed, and he shook his head slowly. He ran a hand through his thick, curly hair. For the hundredth time I wished I'd inherited at least that aspect of his looks. My own straight, shoulder-length blond hair wouldn't hold a curl if its life depended on it.

"Yup. I guess you're right." He didn't sound happy about agreeing with me.

I knew Dad had been hoping that the damage had seemed worse to him at first sight than it really was. He had hoped I'd promise him that a weekend with a screwdriver and a can of paint—or whatever one uses to fix a collapsed ceiling—would take care of the mess.

Since my mom had died two years ago, my dad had really come to rely on me. And most of the time he treated me like an adult, not a sixteen-year-old. I was the one who fixed our dishwasher when it broke. I made sure he got to the dentist every six months to have his teeth cleaned. Everyone who knew him called him the nineties version of the absentminded professor and said how lucky he was to have me.

Unfortunately right now I felt more like a depressed, currently homeless sixteen-year-old than a responsible, mature voice of reason ready to dispense advice. Our home was trashed—and I had no idea where we were going to sleep until everything could be repaired.

But even in the throes of my own misery I still felt horrible for my dad. We had only moved into the new place a few months before. I'd just finished decorating my room exactly the way I wanted it. But my dad had bought all new furniture to celebrate his appointment to full professor at Boston University. Last week he'd finally moved his enormous collection of books out of storage, where they'd been packed away since we'd moved out of our old house.

The storm was a fluke for so early in the summer—and it had been the most punishing hurricane to hit New England in over a hundred years. The storm had caused our quaint old building's roof to practically cave in. And since we lived on the top floor, our penthouse apartment had suffered the worst damage of all.

Water had flooded every room to at least ankle level and had leaked through the floors to the apartments below. The whole building was being evacuated for extensive repairs. I hadn't been inside yet, but I'd heard my dad talking to our landlord from the phone in our hotel room downtown. It didn't sound as though we'd have much to pack up.

"Come on, Dad," I said, trying to sound cheerful. "I'll buy you an ice cream at Herrell's. On me, and you know what a rare occasion that is." I nudged my dad with my elbow.

The few times I'd taken my dad out for lunch or to the movies he'd pretended to faint with the shock of my extravagance. Not that I was cheap or anything, but *one* of us had to be careful about money.

"We can talk about what we're going to do on the way." I nudged him again.

He was still staring at the roof of the apartment building. An expression both sorrowful and perplexed was frozen on his usually happy face.

I was already making plans. Maybe we could move in with Alison and her family. No, their house was packed with stepsiblings and pets. And my dad was deathly allergic to dogs. Better yet, we could stay with my cousins. They lived half an hour out of the city in Sudbury. Thirty minutes wouldn't be a bad commute into Brookline. And my dad didn't get to see his sister, my aunt Sheila, very much anyway. This would be a perfect opportunity for them to spend more time together. But would she want us both to move in for several weeks, maybe even months?

I was so distracted that I barely noticed my dad's pensive frown.

My dad, Professor of Psychology Greg Mazlin, to be exact, is a great dad and generally a very impressive guy. He's good-natured, easygoing, and doesn't hassle me about trivial matters like curfews and spending too much time on the phone.

But he's not great in a crisis. Dad is truly awful at making decisions. My mom used to say that he couldn't even decide which side of bed to get out of in the morning. It doesn't help matters that he is also incredibly absentminded, fairly disorganized, and very lax about maintaining an appointment book.

Clearly I was going to have to come up with a plan. Who knew what crazy setup we'd find ourselves in if I left matters in my dad's well-meaning but undeniably klutzy hands?

I practically had to pull him away from his spot on the curb. Finally he turned away from the building and caught stride with me as we walked up Commonwealth Avenue. It was a perfect summer day, not too hot, not too humid, not a cloud in the sky. This was the kind of day that made me glad I lived in Massachusetts.

Another reason I was glad to be a Boston native was the ice cream. Herrell's has the best ice cream in the entire country, if not the world.

We reached Herrell's and waited in the permanently installed long line for our ice cream—Chocolate Pudding for both of us (always a cone for me, a dish for Dad).

I steered my dad to one of the small tables in the back of the seating area. Before I could tell him my relocation options, he set his dish down on the table and gave me his most serious look.

"Dina, I know you might find this hard to believe, but I've actually been doing a lot of thinking over the past few days." He paused. I had just enough time to experience the lurching feeling I get in my stomach when I anticipate really bad news.

"Actually, Dad . . . ," I began, hoping to cut him off at the pass. His resolve scared me. I had a sinking suspicion that I knew what he was going to say.

"I've decided we're going to move in with Nancy until they can fix up our place," he interrupted.

"But Dad!"

"This is final. Moving in with Nancy is the best thing to do. For both of us."

★   ★   ★

"Ugh, this is disgusting!" Alison held up a pair of pink shorts that had once been her absolute favorites. She had lent them to me only after I'd begged her for a month. And after she'd demanded I lend her the blue cashmere sweater I'd inherited from my grandfather. Now the shorts were completely soaked in muddy water, like just about everything else in my bedroom.

I shot her a pointed look. Alison was one of my favorite people in the whole world, but tact was not her strong suit.

To her credit, Alison looked guilty. She squeezed water out of the dingy fabric into an existing puddle on the floor. "I'm sorry, Dina. I know the hurricane wasn't your fault."

She took a barrette out of her back pocket and twisted her long brown hair into a knot at the top of her head. Her large brown eyes darted around the room, surveying the damage. "I just didn't expect this all to be quite so . . . dire."

I knew Alison felt bad for me. How could she not? And she had volunteered to help me sort through all my stuff without having to be asked.

But packing was the least of my worries at this point. Throwing away half of my possessions paled in comparison to what I was going to have to endure for the rest of the summer. My situation was horrendous. There was no getting around it. My dad and I were going to have to move in with his heinous girlfriend until our apartment was back to normal. I didn't know if I'd survive the experience.

Okay, so Nancy wasn't exactly heinous. To be perfectly fair, she'd been really nice to me the few times I'd condescended to spend time with her. She had even called me on a couple of occasions and invited me to do things with her, just the two of us. But as far as I was concerned, the last thing my dad needed was another woman in his life. Especially Nancy.

"Do you think your dad and Nancy will ever get married?" Alison asked as she filtered through the papers and mementos in my desk drawers.

"Not if I have anything to do with it," I answered quickly. Just because we were going to be temporarily moving in with the woman didn't mean my dad was on the verge of a proposal. Really, Alison watched far too much television. She always jumped to the most melodramatic conclusion possible.

"But they've been going out for a long time," Alison insisted. She held up a small, dark green notebook that appeared to have escaped significant water damage. "Hey, do you want to keep this?"

I jumped up and took the notebook from her. "Yeah, I'll hold on to that." It was my most recently completed diary. I'd been keeping a diary faithfully since I was about ten, and I saved all the old ones. I figured if I ever had a daughter of my own someday, maybe I'd let her read them all so she could learn what I was like as a kid. The idea stemmed from my own regret that my mother hadn't kept a diary. I wished all the time that I'd known more about her life. Now I never would.

"Touchy, touchy." Alison held her hands up in the air. "Don't worry. I'm not going to read it or anything." She paused. "But seriously, maybe your dad is thinking of this move as a premarriage trial period. You know, to help him . . . recover faster."

"He'll never forget about my mom, if that's what you're implying." I knew I sounded angry, but I couldn't suppress my temper when it came to defending my mom. "My mom was his great love. In *my* family we mate for life."

That was a low blow. Even though I was angry, I immediately regretted the words. Alison's parents had been divorced for years. But she just rolled her eyes.

As for me, I was still far too sensitive about the subject of my mom in general, and my father's current love life in particular. I knew it, but somehow I couldn't seem to do anything about it.

"I'm sorry, Al. You know I didn't mean that the way it came out." I tossed a saturated stuffed elephant that she'd given to me for my birthday a few years ago at her feet in a gesture of apology. The elephant landed with a delicate splash. Alison squeezed it out and put it aside with the shorts.

"I *am* worried about you," she said quietly. "You'll be much better off if you try to accept Nancy's presence in your dad's life. I'm sure she doesn't want to become your new mom or anything. My stepmother, for example, has total respect for my real mom and would never want me to think of her as a replacement of any kind."

Alison didn't look up from the pile she was sorting through. Besides the fact that she'd brought up the subject at all, I found it more than slightly annoying that she was plying me with pop-psychology lingo.

"Yeah, whatever." I appreciated her concern, but the last thing I needed right now was a pro-Nancy best friend.

To underline my original assertion about my dad's undying love for my mom, I stood up and gently took my favorite picture of me, Mom, and Dad off the wall. The photo had been taken during a family vacation to Martha's Vineyard.

I remembered this day specifically, in minute detail. My mom had decided we were going to Menemsha, a tiny harbor at one end of the island, to watch the sun set. She'd packed an enormous picnic dinner. We'd driven to the piers, where a few fishermen still stood, hoping to reel in the catch of the day. We had unpacked all our food on an isolated flat rock. Just before we'd dug into our feast, my mom had asked one of the fishermen to take a picture of us.

I felt dangerously close to tears as I examined the picture up close. I'd studied it a thousand times before, searching for clues in my mother's face. I wanted to recapture the remnants of the feeling I'd had that day at Menemsha: the three of us together, a family.

With a defiant flourish I placed the framed photo smack on top of the pile in the plastic crate I was using to collect my most precious belongings.

Take *that,* Nancy.

When I looked up, Alison was watching me. She didn't say a word.

When we were finally preparing to leave the apartment, Alison made one last check of my closet. I stood in the doorway holding the now full crate. Emptied of all our belongings and stained and sagging with water damage, the apartment was incredibly depressing.

"Hey, what's this?" Alison held up a round piece of cardboard I couldn't quite identify from across the room.

I wasn't sure why we needed to stop the proceedings to investigate what looked like a piece of trash. But I set the crate down and slugged across the carpet.

When I got close enough to see what Alison was holding, my heart began to beat fast. How could I have left that behind? I reached out and took the object in my trembling hands.

It was a coaster I'd saved from the lodge restaurant at Mount Blizzard.

For a moment I couldn't speak. My head felt light, and I was suddenly dizzy. Slowly I turned the coaster over. The ink was blurred from the water now, but I could still make out the words.

My name and Matt's, written in my fanciest calligraphy, just as I had remembered. At the bottom of the coaster I had written "Spring break forever." Kind of cheesy, sure, but the words spoke volumes to me now. The souvenir conjured up a week's worth of unforgettable memories.

"Dina, are you there? Earth to Dina!" Alison was snapping her fingers in front of my face. "Either that thing has magic powers or there's a pretty good story behind it." She stood over me, hands on hips, waiting for my response. "I'm waiting."

"It's Matt." I swallowed hard, thinking about what to say next. Of course I'd told Alison that I'd met a guy on the ski trip I'd taken during spring break over a year ago. But I'd also held back when I told her the story. Way back. I had never shared my real feelings about that week with anyone—not even Alison.

The emotions were just too intense. It was still painful to think about Matt. Painful because I missed him so much whenever I thought about him.

"I never told you this before," I said to Alison now. "I think I was really in love with him."

Before Alison had a chance to make one of her patented sarcastic comments—something along the lines of, "Yeah, well, after a whole week you'd think you'd know for sure," I amended my confession.

"Or maybe not in love, but I felt like we could

have been great together, you know? If the circumstances had been different . . ." My voice
drifted off as I remembered the amazing kiss we'd
shared on the mountain.

I'll never forget you, Matt had said. *And someday, sometime, we'll meet again.* I'd believed him,
told him I felt the same way. We had both known,
though, that there was no point in trying to have a
complicated long-distance romance when we'd
basically never get to see each other.

But standing here now, envisioning us in each
other's arms in front of a roaring fire, I couldn't
remember why we'd ever been so dumb.

I missed Matt. I had missed him all year—I'd
just managed to suppress my longing. Part of me
kept hoping he'd find me . . . that what we'd felt
was so powerful, we could never be kept apart.
But nothing like that had happened. And after
losing my mom, I didn't like to spend too much
time dwelling on what could have been. Now I
forced myself to toss the coaster into my crate
with feigned nonchalance.

"What's he like?" Alison asked, sounding
genuinely interested. I felt bad for not having
shared my real feelings with her from the beginning. We made a general practice of telling each
other everything.

"He's like no one I've ever met," I said immediately.

"Not even like Joel Harvey?" she teased,
knowing the perfectly nice, strikingly handsome,

but far-from-magnetic Joel, who'd had an unrequited crush on me since practically kindergarten.

"Way, way out of Joel's league."

Alison looked impressed. Joel wasn't the guy for me, but he was considered quite a catch at Brookline High.

I could tell she wanted to probe me for more information, but we heard my dad calling us from the street, where he was waiting, double-parked, in our ancient orange Volvo station wagon. The horn honked twice and then, after a pause, twice more. I picked up the crate again. Alison took a bag over each shoulder. We walked down the hallway and waited for the elevator. "I don't know how to describe him," I said. "It seems pointless to talk about it now. I'll always remember that spring break as the most amazing week of my life, though." I shifted my weight. The crate felt heavier now that I was standing still. The coaster was on the very top, right next to the family picture. I sighed. Why was life so confusing?

"I wonder if you'll ever see him again." Alison held the elevator door open for me.

"With my luck, probably not."

TWO

MATT

A S USUAL, MY dorm room was a complete and utter pit. I had just spent half an hour trying to find everything I needed for practice—my cleats, jersey, water bottle, and my favorite soccer ball. One cleat had been hidden under my roommate Andy's covers, down by the end of his bed.

Of course, I'd known to look there in the first place because just the day before Andy had found *his* U.S. history book under *my* covers. Whatever someone wanted to say about Riley Prep guys, they couldn't say we were uptight about cleanliness.

I jumped when the phone rang. It was a cordless, and for a change the receiver was right by my head, instead of buried under someone's dirty laundry.

I was sitting on the floor, tying my sneakers extra tight for our prepractice run. I looked at Brandon's digital clock; it was already 3:30 P.M. Should I answer

21

or ignore? The last time I'd been late to practice, Coach Weiant had made me run an extra mile after we had scrimmaged.

If it rings four more times, I'll answer it.

I was always playing little games like that. It was something my mom had done with me when I was growing up. "If it rains before lunchtime, we'll go out for sundaes," she'd say. I'd wait all morning by the window, watching the sky.

The phone kept ringing. Once more, twice more.

On the third ring I picked it up. Oh, well. Who can resist a ringing phone?

"Hey, you ready to chow?" Andy looked up from his omnipresent music magazine as I walked in the room two hours later.

Sometimes I wondered if he even liked reading them anymore or if it had just become a habit.

Andy talked about starting up a band every once in a while, but he couldn't even stay on-key when he was humming along with the radio. And the way he played the guitar made it into an instrument of torture.

Brandon, my other roommate, was in his customary position. He spent hours each day sprawled out on the floor on the phone, talking to his girlfriend in a low voice. They had intense talks about the status of their relationship about four times a day. But after years of being a phone addict, he'd learned to talk and listen at the same time. I knew he'd heard Andy's suggestion to go to dinner when he gave me the thumbs-up signal after pointing to his stomach and rolling his eyes.

"I've got to shower first," I told Andy.

I wasn't entirely sure I felt like dealing with these guys. They were definitely my closest friends at Riley, but they could be really nosy. On the other hand, I definitely needed to talk to *someone*. And if a guy couldn't confide in his best friends, who could he turn to?

Jessica.

Theoretically a guy *should* be able to talk to his girlfriend. But as much as I hated to admit I'd been going out with a selfish whiner, Jessica really didn't care about my problems. She just wanted to know what movie we were going to rent or what she should wear to the next formal. But Jessica was another problem altogether. At the moment I had bigger concerns to think about.

I walked over to my corner of the large, rectangular room and sat on my unmade bed. I knew I looked terrible. I could feel my thick brown hair standing up on end, and my sweat-drenched soccer jersey clung to my chest and back. And I felt terrible too.

My head in my hands, I peered through my interlaced fingers. Andy and Brandon exchanged a worried look. I knew that it was out of character for me to be so moody and mysterious. I guess I was begging for them to ask me if something was wrong.

23

"Hey, man. Is everything okay?" In a shocking display of friendship and concern, Andy threw his crinkled magazine onto a pile of clothes on the floor and sank into the faded armchair by the foot of my bed.

Brandon murmured something unintelligible into the receiver and gently hung up the phone.

"I guess so. No. I don't know." I felt like an idiot, stuttering and contradicting myself at the same time. Better just to spit it out.

"You know, well, I think I told you how my dad and I were supposed to go away camping this summer in Colorado?" They both nodded. "Well, he just found out, I mean he got some news, I mean he's got to go away on business. For the whole summer. To Singapore."

I paused, giving this last piece of dramatic information plenty of time to sink in.

Andy and Brandon exchanged another look, but neither of them spoke.

"So?" Brandon finally asked.

"He says I've got two choices. I can work as a counselor at the camp in New Hampshire I used to go to when I was a kid. Or I can spend the summer in Boston with my mom." I sat up straighter. "What do you guys think I should do?"

As usual Andy spoke first. "Dude, there's no way you're going back to camp."

"He's right, for once in his life," Brandon agreed immediately. Andy smacked him on the head with a pillow. They had this routine down to a science after two years of living together. "Working as a counselor in boring New Hampshire would be a major step backward," Brandon continued. "You should go to Boston. Always choose the unknown over the known."

For a moment I forgot that Brandon usually chose the couch over class, a take-out menu from Napoli's Pizza Palace over the one-hundred-yard walk to the dining hall. But I had to concede that in this case he did have a point. I'd only been to Boston a couple of times. I'd never lived there. And I'd been spending my summers in New Hampshire for what seemed like my entire life.

He's right. The unknown over the known. Take a walk on the wild side for a change, Harbison.

Andy nodded. "And Boston's a real babe fest. High-school girls, summer-school girls, even college girls. Girl, girls, girls. By the way, what are you gonna tell Jessica?"

Andy had a knack for bringing up the wrong subject at the wrong time. As soon as my dad had mentioned the possibility of going to Boston, any residual affection I had for Jessica had dried up. My mind was racing with thoughts of a different girl entirely—Dina Mazlin. But I wasn't about to tell Andy and Brandon that I was harboring sappy feelings for a girl I barely knew.

"Girls, shmirls," I said lightly. "They're all over the place. Especially when you've got my fantastic looks and winning personality."

Andy and Brandon didn't even acknowledge

my lame attempt at a joke. They had both picked up their guitars and started to play an out-of-tune rendition of "Box of Rain," by the Grateful Dead. For once I didn't think about joining in. I was too preoccupied with the million thoughts that were running through my head. Living with my mom. For the first time since the divorce. This could be my first and only real chance to bring my parents back together.

Finally I would be right there to take matters into my own hands, and they'd had enough time apart now—three years—to have started to miss each other big time.

My mom had moved from Los Angeles to Boston almost a year ago, when she'd gotten a job at Boston University. She had bought a house—one room of which she had reconstructed to be an exact replica of my old room in L.A. She'd bought sheets just like the ones I'd had on my bed at home and my favorite sports posters, and she'd even had my dad send her some of my soccer trophies to arrange on the bookshelves. But so far I had only seen photos of the house. I hadn't been to visit even once.

But would my mom even be psyched to have me stay with her? I hadn't talked to her in a couple of weeks. For all I knew, she'd decided to sell her new house in Boston and go on an archaeological dig in Israel. Highly unlikely for a professor of social psychology who specialized in couples counseling, but anything was possible.

These were matters requiring intense, focused

concentration. Andy and Brandon were great for some things, like organizing a rigged poker tournament or getting Napoli's to deliver an extra large with pepperoni at two o'clock in the morning. But concentration was neither's forte.

"Guys?"

Andy and Brandon stopped playing midchord, which was a relief on several levels.

"Yeah?" they said at the same time.

"Go ahead to dinner. I'll be there in ten minutes." I needed some time to collect my thoughts. Not to mention to take a shower. In the last few minutes I'd become painfully aware of my own stench.

Once they were gone, I took a deep breath. Then I picked up the phone and dialed the now familiar Boston area code.

"You're kidding me, right?" The incredibly popular, incredibly snobby, incredibly manipulative Jessica Borg flipped a strand of her perfectly styled blond hair behind her left ear. "You actually think this is funny?"

"No, Jess. It's no joke. I just talked to my mom before dinner, and it's final. I'm going east for the summer."

It's not like she would have seen me that much anyway, I told myself. True, she was from Denver. And my dad and I had planned to make Denver our home base for the summer. But we wouldn't have brought Jessica along on any of our camping excursions. I couldn't imagine her pitching a tent and wolfing down canned beans and hot dogs.

Jessica and I had been "going out," in Jessica's terminology, for just over a month. But sometimes when she talked about our so-called relationship, she made it sound as if we were practically engaged.

"Come on, Jess," I told her over the din of the dining hall chatter. "A summer away from me will be good for you. You can find a boyfriend who has enough money to take you out for dinner, just like you've always wanted. Maybe he'll even buy you jewelry."

Judging from her shocked expression, my comment was a direct hit. Just that morning Jessica had told her best friend Nicole LaBorde (who had told her other best friend, Jenny Bender, who had told Brook Lanford, Brandon's current girlfriend and aforementioned partner in phone crime) that the main problem with Matt was "that he never gave jewelry."

Of course, Brandon hadn't hesitated to pass on the juicy information. Give a girl jewelry? Jeez, I still got an allowance. "I've had it with you, Matt Harbison." Jessica stood up, fuming.

I flinched, hoping she wouldn't throw anything at me or dump a glass of Coke over my head in front of the entire school.

Instead she gave me an evil glare. "You don't deserve me!" she shouted.

Then Jessica turned and stormed out of the dining hall, stomping her expensive leather boots as she left.

"No one deserves that," Andy said from across the table, where he had been unabashedly glued to every word.

"What a she-monster," added Brandon. He popped my last french fry into his mouth. "You've got bad taste in women, Matt. But I must say, that was a pretty entertaining scene."

I groaned. It didn't seem so funny to me. These days nothing did.

Dear Diary,

Well, it's settled. I talked to my mom again tonight. She sounds genuinely excited that I'm coming to stay with her. As usual she brought up the subject of Greg, her new boyfriend. But I told her I really didn't want to talk about him. More and more this summer seems like a great opportunity for me to make her forget about this jerk and realize how much of a loser he is compared to Dad.

Once I'm actually in the house for a reasonable chunk of time, I'll be able to remind her of all the fun we used to have as a family—before all the fighting began. Like the time we . . . well, I guess I can't really think of a specific time off the top of my head. But I'm sure I'll be able to come up with something over the next week. In the meantime I've got to find all my best pictures of Dad and that clipping from *The*

Wall Street Journal where they interviewed him about his new company. That ought to wipe all thoughts of Professor Lamebrain right out of her mind.

And Jessica and I are officially broken up. Not that we were ever really going out, the way I think of going out. But after that one dance when we spent all that time together, she told everyone we were together. I guess because even though so much time had passed, I was still kind of messed up after meeting and losing Dina so fast, I just sort of fell into the whole thing. Unfortunately Jessica is shallow and doesn't have a shred of a sense of humor—about herself or anything else. Okay, so she's hot . . . no one can deny that. But Jessica isn't the kind of girl I'd even want to be friends with. She's nothing at all like Dina, for one thing. Dina was so down-to-earth, so smart, so funny . . . plus she was gorgeous, which doesn't hurt. Wait a minute, what am I doing? I'm writing about Dina in the past tense, like she's dead or something! She's not dead, just gone. Well, not totally gone. She's in Boston. . . .

THREE

DINA

"HON, CAN YOU get out and guide me into the driveway?" My dad was peering into the rearview mirror, trying to back up. With all the stuff we'd salvaged from the apartment piled up in the backseat, he couldn't see.

"Sure," I answered in what I knew was a sulky voice. I hopped out and stood in the street where I could see well enough to prevent my dad from slamming into Nancy's garage door.

I knew I was acting like a jerk, but I just couldn't get myself psyched about moving in with Nancy. I guided my dad with half of my attention. With the other half I scoped out the house. I'd been here once before, when my dad had forced me to have dinner with him and Nancy. That dinner had been painful—full of desperate attempts on Nancy's part to engage me in some capacity.

Nancy knew I wasn't nuts about the idea of her and my dad dating, and I wondered how she really felt about this whole moving-in business. She probably wasn't thrilled at the prospect of a summer with me.

I scanned the wide lawn and the large, white colonial structure. Nancy's house was beautiful but somewhat empty. She said that since her son was still in California, she didn't have a lot of motivation to make her new house into a home.

I could just imagine that kid. Prep school in *California?* Give me a break. The guy's idea of homework was probably looking for shells on the beach.

I was sure that Brookline High was a lot better than Robin Leach's Finishing School for Rich Brainless Jocks or wherever Nancy's evil spawn spent his days and nights. Ugh!

I turned my full attention back to my dad's painfully slow backing-up job.

"Another foot, Dad—okay, okay, stop!" He braked just an inch or so away from the garage door.

For a second I regretted my lost opportunity. I had a sudden vision of Nancy's perfect, white, freshly painted garage door being smashed to bits by my dad's decrepit station wagon.

Just as my dad jumped out of the car Nancy appeared in the front doorway. The image of the car was instantly replaced by one of Nancy wearing a pointy black hat and carrying a broomstick.

What she was actually wearing was a pair of faded jeans, an ordinary navy blue shirt, and gardening boots.

My mom would never have worn shoes like that. She wasn't much of an outdoorswoman. She had always said she would rather be relaxing in the hammock with a good book than kneeling in the mud to pull weeds. She and my dad had talked about books all the time. Who knew if Nancy even liked to read?

Nancy was smiling as she caught my dad's eye. But when she turned and saw the expression on my face, she looked a little bit unsettled.

Good. She ought to be. I'm the family here, not her. Of course, this *was* her house. I pushed the thought away, folding my arms firmly across my chest in what I hoped was a disapproving, fortresslike manner. I couldn't control my father's behavior, but I could sure be responsible for my own.

I knew I was walking a fine line. I wanted Nancy to feel my disapproval, but I didn't want my dad to think I was being rude to her. As she brushed by me I took a pointed step backward to avoid touching her. She didn't seem to notice.

"Oh, my gosh!" she exclaimed as she walked over to the car and saw how much stuff we had brought.

"What?" He made a dopey, embarrassed, apologetic frown and shrugged.

I noticed somewhat nervously that he was still a pretty attractive man—in a teddy-bearish dad kind of way. His eyes were bright blue like mine. *Like Mom's too,* a little voice in my head reminded me. And although he looked a bit scruffy—as usual—he was in great shape for a guy his age. I'd never before bothered to evaluate his appeal on the desirability-to-women scale. I had never needed to.

Convincing Nancy that my dad was a dead-weight was going to be hard.

"Greg, I thought you said everything was ruined!" Nancy exclaimed. "You look like you're moving in for good." The happy grin on her face belied the harsh-sounding words. Nauseatingly enough, my dad gave her a sappy grin.

"You never know," he said. "And if you think this is a lot of stuff, you should see what we had to throw out." He made the remark sound like a joke, but to me it wasn't very funny.

I was the one, after all, who'd had to stop him from throwing out a huge, drenched and filthy pile of my mom's old dresses and sweaters. And it was me who'd had to throw out basically all of my own clothes, most of my books, and virtually all of my photographs.

Nancy gave me a bright smile. "Dina, first things first. Let me show you to your room."

She took my arm with one hand and an over-stuffed canvas bag with my initials on it in the other. I had no choice but to accompany her.

For the tenth time that day I wished that Alison had come along to help unpack. But she had said that she would rather watch the Weather Channel all morning than hang out with me and Nancy in the mood I was in. I couldn't blame her. Already I was feeling sick to my stomach.

"Hang on a sec." I detached myself from her grip. "I've got to carry some stuff too." I took my carefully packed crate in my arms and followed her up the path to the side door of the house.

Upstairs, along the walls of the hallway, were black-and-white photographs. Most of the pictures were of a baby, and then more of what appeared to be the same baby as a toddler, then a small boy.

In one shot the little boy looked directly at the camera, with a smile on his face that was virtually identical to Nancy's. As I stared at the photo I had a funny feeling. Déjà vu. This kid looked somehow familiar. I shook my head. There was no way I had seen Nancy's son before. The hurricane must have messed with my brain.

"Nice pictures," I said to Nancy, more to make conversation than anything else.

"Yes, aren't they great? My ex-husband took them. He's an amateur photographer. I don't know if he still takes pictures . . . but I do know that Matthew doesn't let his father use him as a subject anymore. He thinks it's embarrassing."

I didn't listen carefully to the last part of this

explanation. I was busy examining what was to be my new bedroom.

My initial impression was that I'd never seen such a masculine room. Sports posters were everywhere, virtually papering the walls. What seemed like hundreds of trophies were lined up on bookshelves on three sides of the room. The bedspread was navy-and-red plaid to match the curtains, and a dark green throw rug was centered on the polished pinewood floor.

"This is the room I originally set up for Matt," Nancy explained.

No kidding, I answered silently.

"Actually I think you two would really get along," she added.

I doubted Nancy was right about that, but I managed to keep my mouth shut. Thank goodness her son wasn't going to be around! The last thing I wanted was to spend my summer palling around with Nancy Jr. I was going to have enough to stress out about trying to convince my dad that Nancy was wrong for him. I didn't need to take on a nerd-sitting job as well.

"He's quite handsome," she teased as she headed back down the stairs. "I'll have to get you a more current picture."

"No thanks," I mumbled under my breath.

I leaned against the doorway and stared into my new room. There was nothing I liked more than a redecorating challenge. . . .

★   ★   ★

"Jeez, it's late!" I said out loud, holding up my wrist to look at my watch.

I was all alone in my new room. All morning long I'd been moving furniture around, repostering the walls, and making the bed over with my own freshly dry-cleaned Laura Ashley bedcovers. It was now 1:00 P.M.

Surveying my completed surroundings, I sighed with satisfaction. The room didn't look like home exactly, but it didn't look like alien territory anymore either.

Something's still missing, I thought. I glanced from the dresser to the bed to the closet. *What is it?*

Jumping from the desk chair where I'd been perched, I ran over to the plastic crate, which I had put aside. There it was. The picture of my family. I had saved the picture for last, and I had almost forgotten about it. I wiped the dust from the glass panel covering the photo. Then I hung the picture carefully on a nail above my bed. The finishing touch.

"Dina, come down and have some lunch with us," I heard Nancy yell from the staircase.

As soon as I heard the word *lunch,* I realized that I had been ignoring the gnawing feeling in my stomach. I hadn't eaten all day.

I wasn't thrilled about trotting down to the kitchen like a puppy at Nancy's beck and call. But she had said "us," and I wasn't going to let Nancy have any more time alone with my dad than was absolutely necessary.

When I pushed through the swinging door into the sunny kitchen, I saw that Nancy had set up quite a spread. There was a loaf of French bread, a tray with several kinds of cheese, sliced tomatoes, what looked like homemade lemonade, and another tray with salami, smoked turkey, and chicken breast. I hadn't seen so much food in one place in forever.

Over the past few years my dad and I had memorized the numbers of all our favorite take-out places. Empire Garden, Bertucci's, Boston Market. We both hated to cook. Even on our birthdays we went to Carvel for ready-made ice cream cakes.

Dad walked into the kitchen. He wiped his hands on what he called his "moving pants," an ancient pair of paint-stained khakis that he'd had for as long as I could remember. Nancy was still wearing the old jeans she'd had on to help us unload the car.

I suddenly felt foolish in the clean white denim skirt and new striped, boat-neck sailor shirt that I had changed into—I hadn't wanted Nancy to get any ideas about me as a sloppy, lazy, stereotypical teenager.

"Hey, kiddo," Dad greeted me. "If you're half as hungry as I am, you're going to have to fight me for that salami."

He slid into the seat at the head of the table as though it had been made for him. I was still so transfixed by the food that I almost forgot to be indignant at his possessive attitude.

"Hey, Dad," I responded. "I'm sort of hungry, I guess." I pulled out the chair to his left and sat down. Nancy took the seat across from me and started slicing the bread for sandwiches. My stomach growled.

"Dina, we've got something to tell you," my dad began.

Nancy put a restraining hand on his arm.

"No, let me, Greg. It's really my news. I should be the one to break it." She dusted flour off her hands and passed us each a sub-size hunk of the bread. "Dina, you know that I have a son."

"Sure." I shrugged. I'd seen the kid all over the walls upstairs. Not to mention the fact that she'd brought up the subject every time I had ever seen her, trying to forge some kind of a bond with me. *You're a teenager, I have a teenager, let's be friends, blah, blah, blah.*

"Well, Matthew *had* planned on spending his summer break with his father. They both love to camp out, and his dad was going to take him hiking in the mountains. To Colorado."

I suddenly had a very bad feeling. It was the *had* before the *planned* and the blatantly fake smile on my father's face. Obvious signs that something was amiss.

"But Matt's father has to go on an important business trip overseas instead," Nancy continued. She leaned across the table for a slice of turkey. "So he'll be staying with us."

39

For a moment no one looked up from their plate.

Then I stared straight at my dad. He met my gaze with a worried expression. Nancy rubbed her forehead with the back of her hand.

"I think I'll eat my sandwich out in the garden," Nancy announced.

For a moment Dad and I watched her retreating back. Then I looked back into his eyes. This latest development was too much. This meant war.

I picked up my sandwich too and rose from the table. There was no way I was going to sit there munching on a hero handmade by the woman who seemed determined to ruin my life. But part of me felt sorry for my dad. I could tell he was starting to realize how horrible this whole situation was going to be for me. The look on his face spoke volumes.

But I forced myself to think about Mom. I leaned in close so that Nancy, sitting only a thin wall and several feet away from us on the cedar bench in the backyard, couldn't hear.

"Just what you wanted, Dad," I hissed. "A ready-made family, complete with a sports hero son."

My dad winced. "Honey, let's talk about this rationally. . . ."

I leaned in even closer, ready to go in for the kill. I wasn't going to make this easy for him. I couldn't. "It'll be just like Mom never existed."

★　　　★　　　★

Dear Diary,

Talk about dropping a bomb. All right, I admit I was a little hard on my dad. Okay, I was incredibly mean. But I couldn't help myself. I was just so freaked out by the news that I overreacted. When Dad came up to my room to say good night, he looked horrible—red eyed and exhausted. I was pretending to be asleep, but I caught a good look at him in the hall light. I know that he wants me to be happy. And I know he had no idea about Nancy's kid's change of plans when he decided to move us in with her.

I guess I just never took this relationship with Nancy very seriously. I figured it was just a fling. But flings usually don't last quite so long, especially between friends and colleagues who really respect and admire each other. And flings, from what I've heard anyway, don't usually involve the kids.

I told Dad I would probably like Nancy better if I didn't have to live in her house, but he wouldn't even consider letting me go stay with Alison.

"We're a family, Dina," he said. "We have to stick together."

He looked so unhappy that I promised him I would try. But I can admit to you that I had my fingers crossed the whole time. . . .

FOUR

MATT

As THE PLANE bumped and skidded onto the runway at Logan Airport, I opened my eyes.

Boston.

Groggily I stretched and looked out the round, tiny window. I had been to Boston a couple of times when I was younger—long before Mom decided to make the city her home. From the plane it looked the same as I remembered. Lots of water, lots of buildings.

The monotonous voice of the flight attendant instructed us not to leave our seats until the plane had come to a complete stop. But ninety-five percent of the passengers got to their feet anyway. I watched as they shoved one another aside in a desperate attempt to be the first one onboard to retrieve all his or her carry-on luggage.

Finally the plane stopped, and I lined up with the rest of the passengers. As we filed out of the plane I wondered what it would be like to see my mom again, to live with her for the first time in years.

I found myself smiling as I realized again that this sheer proximity to my mom would give me an excellent vantage point in my ongoing mission to get my parents back together. It would be my primary goal for the summer.

Mom was waiting for me at the terminal, just as she'd promised. Her face was the first thing I saw when I left the tunnel connecting the plane to the airport.

"Matt!" She came running toward me, her purse flying behind her.

"Hey, Mom. Long time, no see." I gave her a big hug. I hadn't realized until this moment just how much I had missed her.

"So how was your flight?" she asked fifteen minutes later.

We were walking out to the enormous parking lot, laden down with all my luggage and athletic equipment—including my primary and my backup tennis rackets, my in-line skates, and my lucky soccer ball, which I never traveled without.

"It was fine. No turbulence. But the food stunk."

Mom smiled. "I'll fix you a snack when we get home."

I felt a pang of anticipation. Or maybe it was

hunger. My mom is an amazing cook. It was one of the points I harped on whenever I was staying with my dad.

"Remember the blueberry pies Mom would make in the summer?" I would ask my dad. Or, "Dad, do you have the recipe for Mom's stuffed mushrooms? Mr. Gelb wants to make them for a dinner party." So far my hints hadn't worked any miracles, but no one had ever called me a quitter.

"Here we are," she said now, thumping the car on its beat-up hood. My mom was still driving the same old green Volkswagen convertible she'd had when my parents were still married. My dad had bought it when he received his first promotion. When they had divorced, he'd let her keep it.

Dad should be here too, I thought. The car was just one small symbol of the love they had once shared. The love they could share again.

The Volkswagen was still a mess inside. I shoved old paper coffee cups under the seat and peeled some soggy papers off the dashboard. We threw my bags in the back, then I slid into the passenger-side seat.

My mother was smart—she had been one of the first female psychology professors to get tenure at Boston University—but she was a certifiable slob. Not too hard to figure out from whom I had inherited that trait. Certainly not from my dad. He was one of those hyperneat, obsessive types. It was one of the things about him that had driven me and my mom crazy when we had all lived under one roof.

"The old girl's still kicking, I see," I commented.

She grinned. "Yeah, she's a good old car. She's my baby." She patted the dashboard. Mom seemed to have forgotten that this had been my dad's car too.

As we headed for the tunnel that Mom said would take us out of the city, Mom looked pensive. We were both quiet.

The situation seemed simultaneously entirely normal and utterly bizarre. For a moment I imagined that he was waiting for us back at the house, ready to take us out to dinner. Of course, the house was in California. And he never would have been home in time for dinner—my dad was a workaholic.

"Pumpkin?" My mom hadn't called me that in years. It was strange, but nice too. Comforting somehow.

"Yeah?" I settled deeper into the sheepskin seat covering.

"I don't want to hedge around this, for your sake and mine. I've got some pretty big news."

My heart sank. Wasn't it too soon for big news? In my mind it was big enough news that I was here in the first place, for three months, no less. What could possibly be bigger news than that?

"You know I've been trying to tell you about

Greg, the man I've been seeing, for months now. Since last winter, in fact."

"Sure, the other psych prof. The space cadet." I tried to keep my voice casual, as though I had about as much interest in Greg as in, say, the pothole situation on the Massachusetts Turnpike.

So far I had managed to learn as little about my mom's so-called boyfriend as was humanly possible. The only piece of information I had managed to retain was that she'd described him as "absentminded, totally unlike Dad." Thus my space cadet insult.

"What about him?" Not that I was worried. If I could score three goals against University in the finals, I was tough enough to handle a dorky professor who had his eye on my mom.

"Well, he's going to be staying with us. For a while."

"What?" I gasped.

I thought for a moment that I had misheard her. This wasn't big news; this was earth-shattering devastation. It had to be a joke. It just couldn't be true.

"He's moving in?" I was shocked. But as was often the case with these "big news" revelations (case in point, the separation, then the divorce), the worst was yet to come.

"He already has. And there's more," Mom continued. "He has a daughter around your age. She'll be staying with us too. Their apartment was ruined in Hurricane Pam."

I had a vague memory of watching the NBA finals in the dorm lounge and seeing a special report come over the national news. Something about a storm that had battered the Northeast, "from Maine to Maryland." I guess Massachusetts fit in there somewhere. When my mom hadn't told me about the hurricane on the phone, I figured the newscaster had blown it out of proportion.

"I know this must come as a real shock to you," she said calmly. "But you have to realize that I tried over and over to prepare you more gently over the phone. You just wouldn't ever let me keep talking once I mentioned Greg's name. And I didn't want to run the risk of having you decide not to come because of this. I've been jealous that your dad gets to see you so much, you know."

"That's because he still lives in California, Mom," I said automatically.

I knew my mom would have to have been insane to pass up the chance for tenure at Boston University. But it still hurt that she had moved so far away. I no longer felt like I had a real home.

"I think you'll really like Greg's daughter. She's sixteen, and she'll be working at Big Beans this summer. It's a very trendy coffee shop near the university. I stop there for coffee on the way to work sometimes." My mom was rambling, but I didn't have the energy to interrupt and tell her that she could forget trying to get me to feel enthusiastic about this situation.

She wanted me to be okay with this ready-made family—to tell her I would become the son Greg had never had, the perfect brother to his kid.

That wasn't going to happen. But I could tell Mom would be crushed if I told her straight out that I had no intention of giving off warm fuzzies to her boyfriend and his daughter.

"No promises, Mom. No promises." Those were the words she had used when I had asked her, years ago, to swear that she and Dad would never get divorced.

I'd never forgotten the words, and from the grim look on her face, neither had she.

By the time my mom turned in the driveway, I felt somewhat calmer. After all, how bad could the situation really be? Maybe it was even for the best that the loser and his geeky daughter would be living in the house. *Keep your friends close and your enemies even closer,* I reminded myself.

I threw my heaviest duffel over my shoulder and followed my mom toward the house. It was even prettier than it had been in the pictures she had sent. We walked through the side door. The kitchen looked the way I had expected it to. Herb plants in the window box, my mom's Far Side calendar on the fridge. The sink, full of coffee mugs and sticky glasses.

I dropped my bag on the kitchen floor. "Hey, I'm going to see if my new room looks as much like my old one as it did in those photographs," I said.

48

"Matt—" my mom called.

But I was already heading up the back stairs. I couldn't wait to see what my new room looked like.

When I reached the threshold of the bedroom I thought was mine, I did a double take. Obviously this wasn't the right place. I walked through the bathroom and looked into the room next door. Hmmm . . . this was definitely the guest room. It looked the same as it had in photographs—unlived in, a little too neat, but relatively cozy.

I walked back into the other room and looked around. What was going on?

My soccer trophies were nowhere in sight. My NBA and NFL posters weren't on the wall as they had been in the photographs. Instead there were the kind of art prints that are sold in museum gift shops. A pink floral bedspread was on the bed. The bed that otherwise looked just like the one I had in California. I walked slowly over to the desk, which I recognized up close as a similar model to the desk I'd had growing up, and sat down on the chair. Even the chair looked like my old desk chair. Something weird was going on.

After a few minutes I heard my mom's footsteps on the stairs. She appeared in the doorway. I just looked at her, slowly shaking my head.

"Matt, I never said this would be easy. But you've got to understand. I didn't know you were coming when they moved in. I gave her the bigger room so she'd be able to have all her things around and feel more at home."

I just stared. There was really nothing to say.

"This isn't exactly easy for me either, hon." She looked so sad that I just couldn't get angry with her.

I walked over and gave her a hug. Two hugs in one day was a bit much for me, but these were unusual circumstances. I'd forgive my mom for almost anything. I knew how much she loved me. And she'd only done what she thought was polite and considerate.

But as for the princess who had dared to mess with my trophy collection . . . I was almost looking forward to our meeting now. I already had a few things I'd like to say to her.

A little later my mom and I stood in the kitchen, fixing ourselves a couple of English muffin pizzas. It was a familiar ritual. I had eaten one of these almost every day after school up until the divorce.

As I opened the oven door to slide in the miniature pizzas, I heard a car pull up in the driveway. Two doors slammed shut and then two voices, a deep man's baritone and a higher girl's soprano, floated in through the open window.

"That's them," my mom whispered. "They're back."

She rushed over to the window, leaving the

refrigerator door open in her excitement. "Now remember, you promised me you would try to be friendly."

The voices got louder. Suddenly a man with shaggy hair that desperately needed to be cut entered the kitchen. He held out his hand for me to shake.

The room seemed to shrink. He was a big guy—tall, with wide shoulders and a booming voice. The virtual opposite of my dad, I noted with displeasure. My dad was small and slender and impeccably dressed and never raised his voice above speaking level.

"You must be Matt. I'm Greg Mazlin. It's a pleasure to finally meet you." He turned and looked behind him.

"And this is my daughter." He reached behind him and literally yanked the reluctant girl into the kitchen. "Matt, meet Dina."

The next few seconds extended forever. Hours could have passed—days, even. Dina and I stared at each other. Her mouth dropped open. I could feel my face grow red and hot.

Suddenly my mom shrieked in excitement.

"Greg, come over here! It's that pair of cardinals I was telling you about." Mr. Mazlin seemed to forget that his daughter and I were standing in the kitchen. He rushed over to my mom's side, and they began to engage in some serious "bird talk." Dina and I just stood there.

As I stared at her familiar, precious face a

hundred flashbacks competed with one another in my mind: Dina skiing sleekly down the mountain, her shoulder-length blond hair streaming behind her. Dina at the opposite end of the couch in front of the lodge fire, writing in her diary as I rubbed her feet after a long day on the slopes. Dina giggling on the chairlift at some stupid joke I had cracked, her blue eyes sparkling. I tried to speak, but no words came out of my mouth. Should I announce that we had already met? Should I say what I was really feeling? Or would "I love you" sound too strong?

Before I had realized it, the moment had passed. Dina reached out her hand.

"Nice to meet you, Matt." She looked calm, but her hand was shaking as I took it in mine.

FIVE

DINA

I HAD NO choice but to call Alison, ASAP. This was a situation for which I had no precedent.

Not only was there a hot guy living in the bedroom next door for the entire summer, he was *my* hot guy. Or my *former* hot guy. Or at the very least the guy with whom I had spent the best week of my life and had thought I would never see again.

This kind of stuff—not that either of us had ever been in a situation quite like this one before—was Alison's specialty. For as long as I could remember, she had been my counselor for *affaires de coeur,* as my French teacher would say.

When I was ten years old, Aaron Caplice kissed me on the playground at recess. Then his brother Nathan—apparently in protest of the kiss—dumped his chocolate milk on my head at lunch. Alison was right there to explain to me the attention-getting machinations of elementary-school boys.

Another time Bryant Palmer asked me to skate with him during slow skate at the roller rink in junior high. Then he left me alone in the middle of the floor while he went off with Kristin Lippert. Who told me that he wasn't good enough to kiss the skates on my feet? Alison.

My hands were still shaking as I dialed her familiar phone number. Fortunately she picked up right away.

"Al?" I exclaimed. "You've got to meet me at Big Beans in ten minutes. The craziest thing has just happened to me. I'll explain when you get there." I didn't even give her time to answer. I was pretty confident that her innate curiosity would get her to our favorite coffee bar in five minutes flat.

I could hear Matt and his mom in the guest room, unpacking his stuff. I couldn't make out the words, but the sound of his voice alone was enough to transport me back to spring break a year before. Colorado. I almost felt cold, even though this was the hottest June on record.

"Dina, have I told you that I've never met anyone like you before?" We were sharing an order of curly fries in the lodge café after a day of skiing and snowboarding in the intense Aspen sun.

"About fifty times," I said seriously. "But more important, have I told you that I think you're absolutely perfect?" We were holding hands, which made eating the fries a slow process, but neither of us wanted to let go.

"Only about forty times," he said. "I think I'd like to hear it ten more times if that's okay with you. Then we'll be even." I squeezed his hand. There was no one else in the lodge, no one else at the mountain. It was just us, Matt and Dina, against the world.

I had never felt so perfectly happy in my entire life. I remember wishing that feeling could last forever. For a moment I stood in the hallway outside the doorway to Matt's room. I took a step closer, careful not to let the wooden floorboards creak. I couldn't imagine what could be more embarrassing than being caught eavesdropping on Matt and his mom in their own house.

"He just seems like kind of a loser, Mom," I heard Matt say. "I mean, he's so, I don't know . . . messy."

"Oh, unlike you and me, I suppose." Matt laughed at the comeback. I smiled too, from my precarious position right on the other side of the door. Matt was a slob; even I knew that. When we'd been skiing, he would always lose a glove or his sweater would be on inside out underneath his ski jacket. I was so warmed by the memories of that week that I almost forgot to be angry that Matt had insulted my dad.

"Okay, okay. Point taken." Matt wasn't about to stop there, it seemed. "But he's so loud. And doesn't that stupid laugh get on your nerves? He's nothing like Dad."

Nice. Matt met my dad exactly fifteen minutes ago, and he's already dissing him.

"Well, I guess that's the idea." Nancy's voice sounded a little strained. "Nothing like your father." Apparently she didn't appreciate Matt's probing.

It was weird to hear Matt talking to his mom about my dad. Even though I was annoyed that Matt was putting down Dad, I identified with him. I knew why. The way he felt about my dad was precisely the way I felt about his mom.

I checked my watch. Alison would be at Big Beans in five minutes if all went according to schedule. I had to get going. Part of me wanted to stay and find a way to be alone with Matt. I couldn't think about anything else. But I knew deep inside that I had to get out of there, fast. I would go crazy if I couldn't tell Alison what was going on.

I tiptoed down the stairs. I was almost out the front door when I heard my dad's stern voice boom out from behind me. He stood in the doorway of the kitchen.

"Where exactly do you think you're going?" He didn't look happy, so I decided to play dumb.

"I'm just going out to meet Alison for a cup of coffee. We've been planning it all day." I smiled my most innocent smile.

"You girls see each other twice a day at a minimum. I think you should stay in so we can all spend time together—me, you, Nancy, and Matt."

I rolled my eyes—just for show. I was afraid the fact that all I had wanted to do for over a year was spend time with Matt Harbison was written all over my face. But right now I needed to get my head together.

Dad frowned. "If you really have to go, you should at least invite Matt. He'd probably love to start making new friends."

My dad didn't look like he was about to back down. But neither was I. We stood as if we were in a face-off, old Western style.

"I bet you'll like Matt if you'll just give him a chance," he pleaded. "Nancy says he's a great kid, and from the sound of it, you have a lot in common. He even loves to ski."

I almost burst into laughter. Or tears—it could easily have gone either way. If he only knew . . .

"Dad . . . ," I began tentatively. I wasn't used to keeping secrets from my father. We had a kind of unwritten agreement that no matter what, we would always be as honest with each other as we possibly could.

"Yes," he prompted, after we'd stood for several seconds in utter silence.

"Never mind," I said finally. I just couldn't find the words. Besides, I wasn't sure if there was a point in sharing all this history when I didn't know if Matt and I even had a future.

"Now about meeting Alison." My dad put his hands on his hips, but he didn't look quite so stern anymore. I decided to take a chance. Carpe diem, as Alison was fond of saying before she did anything stupid.

Without any more chitchat, I ran out the front door. "Be back tonight!" I yelled through the open door as I ran for my car. I could deal with the ramifications of such a rash move later. For now I had to get an objective—okay, a totally biased—opinion from one Alison Phoenix.

"What took you so long?" Sure enough, Alison was already sitting at our favorite window table when I pushed open the heavy door of Big Beans several minutes later.

"I'm five minutes late; give me a break!" I held up my watch. "How did you get here so fast anyway?"

"I was out the door before I'd even hung up the phone," she said. "This sounded too good to wait." I looked her over. It wasn't hard to believe she had left her house in a hurry.

Alison's hair was disheveled, tied up in a loose knot, and her lipstick was smudged, as though she'd run out the door without looking in the mirror first. On her, the so-called messy look worked. She blended well into the rest of the crowd at the coffee bar, more college students than high-school kids.

Ever since Alison and I had gotten our driver's licenses, we had been hanging out at Big Beans. We met at the coffee shop at least twice a week after school—more if a crisis came up. And this was definitely a crisis.

We both liked the idea of drinking coffee more than we actually liked the taste of it, so we had developed a lengthy list of available alternatives. We ordered everything from hot chocolate and mulled cider in the winter to the wide variety of summer options the place had designed with customers like us in mind.

But the best thing about Big Beans was the fact that the owners let people linger at the tables for as long as they wanted. No one made us feel guilty for taking up space.

I was really psyched that I had managed to get a part-time summer job there. Even though I had to finish the last couple weeks of school before I started work at Big Beans, I was already starting to feel proprietary about the place.

Before sitting down, I gazed up at the menu. The day's specials were written on a giant chalkboard on the wall above the coffeemakers.

"I already got you a Frozen Mocha." Alison pointed at the extra-large-size paper cups on the marble table. She pulled out an empty wrought-iron chair for me. "So sit down already. I'm dying to hear what's going on."

I sat down, taking a long sip of the slushy drink before saying a word. Alison drummed her nails impatiently on the table as I drank.

"I won't torture you," I said. But then I paused. I wasn't even sure where to begin.

"Guess who moved in next door?" I finally said.

Alison look confused. "Next door to what? Your old apartment?"

"Nope. *Literally* next door. To my new *bedroom*." I raised my right eyebrow at Alison, a trick I used with discretion to enforce any particularly crucial point.

Alison looked confused. "Dina, you're going to have to help me out here. I have no idea what you're getting at."

"Remember I told you about Matt? The guy I met skiing?"

"Yeah." Alison looked even more confused.

"Well. You'll be meeting him after all."

Her mouth dropped open. She put her moccachino back down on the table. "You're kidding me, right?" Her voice was uncharacteristically calm.

"Would I make a joke about the love of my life?"

Finally the reality of the situation seemed to sink in. She actually shrieked. Everyone in Big Beans stared at us. I glared back until the other customers looked away. I met Alison's eyes. "I can't believe it." She shook her head. "*He's* the spoiled prep-school brat you were so worried about?"

We grinned at each other. I could feel my cheeks turning red.

"What should I do?" I asked. "I didn't think Matt and I would ever see each other again!"

"Wait a second," Alison commanded. "Slow down. Way down. How in the world did this happen? You must have a guardian angel or something." She shook her head in disbelief.

"But seeing Matt is complicated." I could feel my expression transforming into an ugly grimace almost entirely on its own. "He's Nancy's son, after all. And we both know how I feel about Nancy."

"What did your dad say about all this?" Alison knew better than anyone how involved my dad was in his only daughter's life.

"That's kind of the problem," I admitted, chewing on the cuticle of my index finger. Whenever I was stressed out, my nails were history.

"What do you mean?" Alison took a long sip of her moccachino. "He doesn't like Matt?"

"No, it's not that," I hedged, stirring my straw around the ice cubes at the bottom of my drink.

"He doesn't like the idea of his precious Dina sharing a bathroom with a cute guy?" Alison wiggled her eyebrows suggestively.

"He doesn't know that Matt and I already know each other," I said quietly.

Alison narrowed her eyes. "And Nancy?"

I shook my head. "She doesn't know either."

"How did you ever work this out?" Alison's eyes were wide and . . . impressed?

She was acting as if I had rigged the whole situation to get Matt to come to Boston and live in the bedroom next door to mine. She clearly didn't understand the complicated nature of what was going on.

"Look, I'm not really all that psyched." I paused. "Okay, I guess part of me is psyched. But I mean, you *know* how I feel about Nancy."

"But why didn't you figure it out? Didn't you ever get Matt's last name down during the week you spent together *in love?*"

I ignored the heavily sarcastic inflection on the last two words of her question. "Matt has his dad's last name—Harbison. Nancy's last name is Weir. And he probably didn't tell her about me at all. Besides, they weren't dating when Matt and I met."

"Amazing," Alison commented.

I nodded. "When they introduced us today, we were both so freaked out that neither of us said a word. We just shook hands as though we had never met before."

For once in her life, Alison was speechless.

I had finally managed to really shock her. But I couldn't even enjoy the moment of glory. I was too confused.

"So what am I going to do?" I asked. Alison's silence was unnerving.

She shrugged. "I don't know, Dina. I just don't know."

Dear Diary,

I feel like my head is about to explode! It turns out that Nancy's son is the guy I fell in love with on the slopes last spring break! Now we'll be living right next door to each other, sharing a bathroom (pause while I imagine him wearing nothing more than a towel—just kidding), and living like brother and sister. Yeah, right.

Let's see, is there anything else crazy about my life? Where do I start? How about the fact that his mother is my current public enemy number one? At the very least I want her and Dad to break up. How about the fact that I have no idea where Matt and I stand as a couple? I mean, we haven't so much as spoken in over a year.

Our week together was like an out-of-time experience or something. Part of what made it so magical was the fact that we both knew at the end of the week, we would go back to our old lives.

For all I know, he has a serious girlfriend now. If that's the case, I might go truly nuts.

SIX

MATT

I WATCHED MY mom as she folded my sweaters and T-shirts into piles on my bed. She looked the same as she had the last time I had seen her, at Christmas, when she had come out to California to visit her sister and hang out with me.

Actually she looked even better. I couldn't pinpoint the change, but maybe *happier* was the right word.

For a second a picture of Mr. Mazlin flashed into my mind. Last winter had been about the time they had started dating. I remembered hearing her and my aunt talking and giggling about how funny it was to go on dates at the age of forty-five.

"Mom," I ventured hesitantly.

"Yes?" She must have sensed a mother-son talk coming on. She pushed a pile of sweaters to the side of the bed and sat down. She looked at me expectantly.

For a moment I lost my courage. "I'm really glad to be here," I said finally, stalling for time. "We haven't spent this much time together in years."

My mom smoothed her short, dark blond hair with one hand. She gave me a look. I knew that look. In fact, I remembered it all too well. She wasn't buying my togetherness speech.

"Um," I began again. "Dad wanted me to be sure to send you his regards." As soon as the words were out of my mouth I regretted them. *Regards* sounded so formal.

My mom just gave me that look again. That mom look that mothers everywhere seem to have perfected.

"I mean, he sent his greetings." Was that even worse? It sounded as though my dad were an alien spaceship landing on my mom's planet for a brief stopover. Greetings from Vulcatron. Why, why, why was I such a moron?

Mom smiled and patted the spot on the bed next to her, pushing another pile of clothes aside as she did so. I sat down next to her. In spite of my misery I had to admit it was nice to be hanging out with my mom again.

Although it had been my choice to go to boarding school—I didn't want to have to choose between my parents—sometimes I really missed the feeling of being at home.

Even though most of my stuff was there, my

dad's ultramodern, spartanly decorated apartment in the nicest part of San Francisco certainly didn't feel like home . . . without my mom. And this was the first time I had even been to my mother's house. And as much as I missed Andy and Brandon—even thought of them as the brothers I had always wanted—there was no way I'd call my tiny, brick-walled dorm room in Strong House at Riley Prep anything even resembling a home. I sighed loudly.

"Matt, I know we've both told you this be-fore, but you can't put yourself in the middle of your father's and my relationship," Mom said, her voice serious. "We both love you more than anything in the world, and it's not your fault that we weren't right for each other. You've really got to come to terms with that."

I nodded, afraid to speak.

Somehow, no matter how old I got, I just couldn't get used to the idea of my parents not being together. The divorce still seemed so wrong to me. The "if onlys" started crowding my thoughts whenever I let myself think about the di-vorce. If only I had been a quieter child. If only I had eaten my spinach without complaining. If only I had gone to bed at a reasonable hour without a fuss. The more ridiculous the equation, the worse I felt. If only I had done *something*.

"The thing is, Matt, I really like Greg. I never thought I would meet anyone else I liked so much." My mom squeezed my shoulder for emphasis.

Anyone else. That sounds promising, I thought.

At least she's acknowledging that she once loved Dad.

"We have a lot in common," she went on. There was a soft, faraway look in her eyes that made me worry. I turned away as she continued. "I never imagined how great a relationship with someone who really respects what I do would be. We're really on the same wavelength when it comes to most important issues, personal and professional. Greg even likes working in the garden."

My father had hated working in the garden. He had thought it was a waste of time when we could get such great vegetables at the local Bread & Circus.

"Are you listening to me, Matt?"

I had been getting tenser and tenser as she spoke, forbidding her words to penetrate my consciousness. I forced myself to imagine my dad, sitting in a dingy hotel room somewhere in Singapore, crying over a faded black-and-white picture of my mom he'd had forever.

I nodded so that she would know I had heard her.

"It's extremely important to me that you and Greg get to know each other. I hope someday you'll even be able to say that you like him." She paused. "But in the meantime I expect you to be friendly and polite. To Greg *and* to Dina."

I knew Mom couldn't see my face, so I didn't bother to conceal my frown. It was clearly going to be up to me to fix my parents' broken marriage. Greg Mazlin was just another obstacle in my path.

But Dina was another story entirely.

Friendly and polite? To the girl of my dreams?

Or the girl who had been the girl of my dreams before I knew her father was the stepfather of my nightmares.

For a moment I considered telling my mom the whole story. Spring break, the mountains, the snow, Dina . . .

Then I thought about that handshake Dina and I had shared this afternoon. The chemistry was still there. Maybe I should talk to Dina privately before I came clean about our so far hidden past.

"Mom?" I said.

"Yes?" she responded.

I could tell by her tone of voice that she was expecting a protest. But I was determined to keep my cool—at least for the time being.

"About Dina."

"Uh-huh." She sounded wary.

"What does she do for fun around here anyway? I mean, for the summer," I asked.

"She's got that job at the coffee shop. Apparently it's quite the place to be. But for now she's still got a couple weeks of school left."

"Hmmm." It was a good sign that Mom hadn't mentioned a boyfriend. But I didn't want to appear too interested. At least not yet. A guy couldn't tell his own mother everything. I jumped off the bed.

"I gotta go, Mom. I'm going to check out the neighborhood and stop by that sporting goods store we passed on our way in from the airport."

As I grabbed my wallet from my desk and

jammed it in my back pocket, I couldn't resist one last comment. "You know, just before he dropped me off at the airport to come east, Dad told me that he misses you."

I ran out of the room before Mom could react.

Dear Diary,

You're not going to believe this one. I can hardly believe it myself. If I watched the scene that unfolded in Mom's kitchen today on TV or at the movies, I would have laughed. Ready? As it turns out, the original Wife Stealer himself (and that would be one Greg Mazlin) is the actual father of the only girl I've ever really cared about.

When Dina and I said good-bye, I wasn't sure I would ever see her again. I mean, I hoped I would. Of course, I thought about her more than I'd like to admit. But we had agreed not to contact each other, to let destiny run its course. We hadn't even exchanged addresses.

The last thing I expected was that the next time we saw each other it would be in my mom's kitchen, being introduced to each other, or rather reintroduced, by our very own parents! There's no way I'm going to be able to get to sleep tonight, knowing she's just a few feet away from me, sleeping in what was supposed to be my bed.

When we first saw each other, standing

there as if no time had passed, I could tell what she was thinking, word for word. I could see my expression mirrored on her face. We were both so shocked, so dumbstruck.

We shook hands, for a moment longer than necessary, and I felt in her touch everything I needed to know. But then as soon as I recovered, she was gone. Her dad seemed embarrassed when he told me she'd had to go out and meet a friend.

But I understood. It was too much, too soon. But then when she didn't come back to the house all afternoon and called to say she wouldn't be back for dinner, I was confused. Didn't she want to talk to me too?

Now so much time has gone by that the very thought of communicating with her in person terrifies me. What will we say? What is there to say? This is either destiny or our worst nightmares come true. I mean, it's not as though I want Greg Mazlin to become any more a part of my life than he already is. And from what I remember about the way Dina feels about her mom, I'd bet she's with me a hundred percent on that subject.

Still, if I get any sleep at all, I know what I'm going to dream about. . . .

I knew it was 11:30 P.M. when I heard the faint opening notes of David Letterman's theme song on the mini-TV in my room. I had been lying in bed, writing in my journal for about half an hour with the volume on low, but I was getting tired. It was time for bed.

But someone had just started running the water in the bathroom between my room and Dina's. Who was I kidding? Someone. Obviously the person was Dina. I wondered what she was doing up so late when she had school the next morning. Then I wondered if she knew I was up too.

I sat up in bed, my mind racing. Should I risk talking to her? What would I say? What *could* I say? Suddenly wide awake, I jumped up and walked over to the bathroom door. Adrenaline pumped through my veins.

I knocked softly at first, then louder. When Dina still didn't respond, I called out, softly enough that our parents wouldn't hear me. "Dina? Is that you?"

The water stopped. After a few seconds passed, the door opened a crack. Dina's beautiful face looked freshly scrubbed. Her silky blond hair was damp, held off her forehead with a black band. She was holding a toothbrush in one hand.

She looked perfect.

"Hey." Dina smiled shyly at me. I had dreamed about that smile during the months since our spring break together. I could barely move, I was so transfixed. Finally I snapped back into reality.

"Please come in." I gestured toward the beanbag chair in the corner of my room, realizing how formal the words sounded as soon as they had escaped my mouth.

"One second." She held up her toothbrush. "I'm almost done."

I went back in my room and tried to arrange myself casually on my bed. I grabbed a couple of car magazines Brandon had lent me for the plane ride off my bedside table and stuffed them under the bed. Somehow I thought they gave the wrong impression. Immature. Unsophisticated.

A minute later Dina came in. For an instant she just stood there in the doorway. She looked nervous. Then I stood up too. Suddenly there was no space between us, and we were in each other's arms. But somehow it didn't feel as though "no time had passed," like they say in the movies. It felt . . . awkward. Like hugging a stranger. We let go at the same time, and I felt a twinge of relief.

Then Dina flopped down on a chair in the corner of the room. She had removed the black headband, but otherwise she looked the same. Amazing. It was the old Dina after all.

"Dina—" I began.

"Matt—" We spoke at exactly the same time. Then we both laughed. I felt the tension start to break.

"You first," I said. The words practically fell out of her mouth.

"What on earth have you been up to? What are you doing here? I can't believe we haven't spoken in over a year! This is the craziest thing that's ever happened to me." Dina shook her head. She looked overwhelmed.

"You're telling me! But one question at a time." I smiled to show her I was teasing.

"Seriously, though. I thought Nancy's son was going to be a total dork." Dina put her hand over her mouth. "I mean . . ." She blushed as she groped for a way out of the comment.

"No, it's okay. I thought you were going to be . . . someone else too. But I'm glad you're not." I gulped as Dina brushed a lock of hair off her cheek. She looked so gorgeous. It was hard to believe she was sitting in my bedroom.

"Our apartment was ruined in the hurricane," Dina explained. "My dad decided this would be the best plan for now."

"I know," I answered. "My mom filled me in this morning on the way back from the airport. I was supposed to go camping with my dad this summer. It's been a long year at school—you know, SATs, trig, we made the finals . . ." My voice faded off. I felt stupid making conversation. We had more to talk about than math and soccer.

"What are we going to do about this?" I asked.

Dina looked as confused as I felt.

"We can't tell them," I said, meaning our parents. "Can we?"

She shook her head. "I don't think so. Not now that we pretended we had never even met."

I nodded. "They might make you move out."

The horrifying thought of losing Dina as soon as I had found her had occurred to me as we had shared that misleading handshake. "Or make me go back to California."

Dina looked thoughtful. I would have given anything to know what was going on inside her head. Her silence was making me nervous.

"Worse yet, our parents might be *happy* about our . . . uh, past," I continued. "And to be totally honest, I'm not nuts about the idea of my mom with your dad."

I took a deep breath. All my fears had spewed out in one long monologue. Now I was exhausted.

Dina leaped off her chair. She crossed the room and plopped down beside me on the bed. "I know, isn't it horrible? It's like your mom has my dad under some kind of a spell. He doesn't even talk about my mom that much anymore. It's like he's forgetting her." She sighed. "What are we going to do?"

I was slightly annoyed by this portrayal of my mom as an evil sorceress, casting spells over Greg Mazlin. But I let the comment slide for the moment. In fact, I let everything slide for the moment.

I hadn't been so close to Dina in what seemed like forever. She was sitting Indian-style on my bed, her long legs folded under her. I could smell her lemony shampoo, her minty toothpaste. I breathed in deeply. Ahh. Heaven.

"I think we should keep our . . . relationship a secret for now. At least until we sort out what we're going to do. There's no sense making complications if we don't need to. We can always pretend we've fallen in—"

I broke off, realizing what I had been about to say. Fallen in love. Here in my mom's house. Was that what we were? In love?

Suddenly Dina and I were looking into each other's eyes. All of the talk about our parents seemed irrelevant.

"Dina," I began tentatively.

"Yeah?" She was still gazing at me.

"We haven't seen each other in a long time. Are you . . . seeing anyone?" I felt stupid asking her—and I sure didn't want to get into the whole Jessica situation—but I had to know.

"Oh, Matt." Dina stood up. "Ever since I met you . . ."

Time itself seemed to stop as we moved slowly toward each other. Her lips met mine. The next instant her arms were around my back, her hands in my hair. Dina's lips were as soft and warm as I had remembered. My heart pounded so loudly, I thought it might explode right out of my chest.

I held Dina close, not wanting to ever let go. I put my hands to her cheeks, her shoulders, her waist. Jessica, who had never felt that real anyway, seemed like a ghost. This was where I was meant to be, who I was meant to be with.

We were still kissing when the sound of Mr. Mazlin's boisterous laugh rang out in the hallway outside my bedroom.

"Kids? Are you guys awake?" Mr. Mazlin's voice was as booming as ever. I heard a higher-pitched laugh. My mom was with him!

Dina jumped off my bed and sprinted through the bathroom and into her room. She didn't even say good night.

I picked up my book and opened it to somewhere in the middle. My door opened, and the happy couple entered. They walked over to the bathroom door so they could talk to us both at the same time.

Close call. My heart was beating so fast, I thought I'd have a heart attack at the tender age of seventeen.

I looked down and noticed that I was holding my book upside down. Quickly I flipped it over.

Mr. Mazlin cleared his throat. "We've planned a group excursion for the weekend. No one make any plans for Sunday, okay?"

I didn't hear Dina's response, meaning it was likely there hadn't been one. My mom was glaring at me, so I nodded weakly. What was I getting myself into?

When I came downstairs the next morning, Dina was already up. She looked like I felt—tired. I doubted that either of us had gotten much sleep the night before.

Dina was huddled over a full bowl of cereal. Her lab notebook was open in front of her on the table. She was so intent on the experiment, she barely looked up when I entered. I opened the fridge to take out the milk for my cereal, but when I lifted the container, it was suspiciously light. I shook it. Sure enough, it was basically empty. Okay. I would just have to have toast.

I popped a couple of slices into the toaster and sat down across from Dina. For the first time she looked up from her bowl of cereal.

"I'm sorry about last night," she said quietly, without meeting my eyes. "I guess I just panicked. I'm not used to kissing someone while my dad's standing right outside the door."

"I know. It's a crazy situation." The toaster popped. I got up to grab my slices.

I wasn't sure what else there was to say. Everything seemed awkward and stilted between us now. Before, our conversations had always seemed so natural. Part of me wanted to bring our parents into the kitchen and confess my love for Dina right then and there. Another part of me rebelled against the very idea. There were just so many "what ifs." As I munched thoughtfully on my toast Dina rapped the edge of her cereal bowl with her spoon.

"Earth to Matt, Earth to Matt."

I looked up. She was smiling at me, which was preferable to avoiding my face altogether like she'd been doing before. But it was an uneasy smile. "The truth is, Matt, I was up all night thinking about us. . . . When you get right down to it, we really don't know each other that well. I mean, the week we spent together was, well . . ."

"I know. You don't have to say it. I feel the same way." I knew what she was getting at; I just wasn't sure I wanted to hear the rest, even if I agreed with her.

Apparently I had no choice. "All I want to say is that I've had a lot of time to think about our relationship now." She rubbed the circles under her eyes as if to stress this point. "And I agree with you. About keeping this—us—quiet for the time being. Let's see what happens before we involve *them.*"

Although I was a tiny bit disappointed that she hadn't vetoed my plan and insisted that we proclaim our love to the world at large, I could see the sense in her words. After all, she was only reiterating what I had told her last night.

But no matter what either of us said, actions spoke louder than words.

And if last night's kiss was any indication, this romance was far from over.

SEVEN

DINA

WITH A FLOURISH my dad pulled a bottle of nonalcoholic sparkling cider out of his bulging knapsack.

"The perfect touch to a perfect afternoon," Nancy said. She saluted my dad with a raise of her plastic wineglass and an approving smile.

I looked over at Matt and his mom. They were leaning against a big rock, side by side. Matt looked so attractive in his red Patagonia hiking shorts and big woolly socks that I had to stop myself from leaning across the picnic cloth and kissing him. Even Nancy looked kind of cute, I grudgingly admitted to myself. Her short wavy hair was tied back in a bandanna, and she was wearing a faded Berkeley University sweatshirt that must have been twenty years old.

There was no doubt about it. We'd had an

ideal day. The sun was shining, but it had grown comfortably cool as we'd climbed higher and higher. And it wasn't over yet. After lunch we were going to keep hiking up to the top of Nobscot Mountain, a relatively challenging climb out in Sudbury. I hadn't been there in ages, so when my dad and Nancy had suggested the day trip, I'd been filled with a sense of nostalgia. And a sense of excitement and fear. This would be the first day the four of us had spent as a group.

I wouldn't let myself use the word *family*, even to myself. I didn't want to give anyone any ideas.

The only problem so far was that Nancy and my dad were so gung ho on the togetherness aspect of the weekend that Matt and I had barely had a second alone. And it wasn't as though we wanted to spend too much time in the company of our parents. In fact, we hadn't been alone, just the two of us, since the other night when we had kissed in Matt's room.

I felt his warm brown eyes on me and glanced up. The expression on his tanned face spoke volumes. Again I felt conflicted. I wanted to be alone with Matt, but I was afraid to acknowledge my feelings. So much time had passed since our perfect week together.

"Dina, do you want to go check out that stream those mountain bikers told us about?" Matt was giving me a look that said, "Don't say no." The idea of going off by ourselves was both appealing and nerve-racking.

When we had been alone before, we had fallen into each other's arms within about two minutes. Was that what I really wanted? And what did another kiss between us mean for the future? Then again, who ever knew what would happen at any given point in time? I would never have thought that Matt and I would end up in the same state, let alone the same house.

I nodded to myself. Obviously sometimes I thought too much. All Matt had asked was if I wanted to go for a walk. And I *did* want to go for a walk, if only to escape the disgustingly mushy looks my dad was exchanging with Nancy.

"Sure," I said.

My dad patted me on the back. "You guys go. We're fine here alone."

I just bet you are, I thought, picturing them happily making out while we got lost in the woods. I was Little Red Riding Hood and Nancy was the Big, Bad Wolf.

Matt and I walked in virtual silence all the way up a little path that veered off the main trail and wove through the dense woods. At one point Matt held the heavy branches back while I walked through. A minute later I warned him when I saw a ripe-looking patch of poison ivy. But for the most part he appeared as lost in his thoughts as I was in mine.

At the stream Matt immediately started skipping stones. "You've got to find the flat ones," he explained without looking up from the pile he was picking through.

As a matter of fact, I already knew how to skip stones. I even considered myself something of an expert. Matt flung a long, pinkish stone downstream. It bounced in the water three times. We both watched the ripples as the stone finally sank. With perfect wrist motion I flicked a gray piece of slate in its wake. I managed four bounces.

"Not bad," Matt said approvingly. I smiled at him. Why did being with him feel so good? Even when we were doing something as mindless as skipping stones. The fluttering in my stomach made me lose all sense of what was rational and sane.

For about fifteen minutes we kept skipping stones. We alternated throws, first Matt, then me. By the time we stopped, we were both getting five bounces on most throws. I hadn't felt so comfortable with anyone in a long time.

"Practice makes perfect," I said as Matt cheered for himself on his first six bouncer.

I hadn't meant my words to have a double meaning, but suddenly I was breathlessly conscious of how close we were standing. The sleeve of his windbreaker touched my elbow. He'd stripped off his socks and hiking boots. I had removed my Tevas and placed them up on the shore. We were standing barefoot, side by side in the shallow part of the stream.

"Dina." Before I knew what was happening, his hands were on my shoulders, his lips on mine.

Standing in the icy, ankle-deep water, our kiss seemed like a continuation of the one we had shared the other night. My heart raced. Matt's arms held me close, then closer. Finally we broke apart.

"Wow," Matt breathed. "That was some kiss."

I just sighed with contentment. Matt kept his arms around me, holding me in a loose hug. I rested my head against his shoulder. I couldn't remember the last time I had felt so happy to be alive.

As I stood in Matt's arms I noted the expanse of blue sky above us, the deep forest all around us. I felt so light, I almost thought I would rise off the ground.

"I want this moment to last forever," I whispered into Matt's shoulder, so softly I didn't think he had heard.

But he had. Keeping his hands on my shoulders, Matt pulled away so he could see my face. "Dina, what are we going to do?" He looked scared and elated and confused all at the same time.

I shrugged. Right now I was so happy that I couldn't muster up any worry about the future. "We'll figure something out."

Suddenly I heard the faint sound of my father's voice. Looking down at my watch, I realized that we had been gone for quite a while.

"We better go," Matt whispered.

I nodded. But somehow I couldn't get my feet to move. Once we returned to the picnic site, and our parents, and all the problems that mess entailed, the magic would be gone. And who knew when or if we would ever get the magic back?

★   ★   ★

At eight P.M. I sat down at my desk and opened my chemistry textbook. I was settling in for a long night of hard-core studying. The day's hike, as fun as it had been, seemed to have happened years ago. Already the kiss Matt and I had shared seemed like an idyllic memory.

I knew I should have spent the afternoon alone at the library, but the opportunity to be alone with Matt had been worth any sacrifice. It was a good thing my dad didn't know how much trouble I was having this semester in chemistry, or he would never have made the plans for the hike. I smiled, remembering the feel of the water swirling around my calves, the sun beating down on my face. The kiss.

Yes, it had been worth it. I had no regrets.

But tomorrow was my chemistry final, my last exam of my junior year of high school. My grade would be the deciding factor determining whether or not I would make the honor roll. The upcoming exam demanded my full attention. I commanded myself to stop daydreaming.

Chemistry was by far my worst subject. My lab partner, an outgoing Swedish exchange student named Inga Webb, had been helping me after class for weeks. But I still hadn't mastered many of the formulas. With a big bottle of diet Coke by my side and a one-pound bag of peanut M&M's on my desk, I was ready for an all-nighter. Thank goodness for caffeine. I was exhausted.

As I finished sharpening my pencil in my

electronic sharpener a loud blast of music jarred me into a state of alertness.

"Oh, the women are smarter in every way. . . ." It was the Grateful Dead. Or rather it was Matt, providing me with an unsolicited concert as he sang along—loudly and way out of tune—to the Dead on his CD player.

I winced at the lyrics. *This* woman was not going to be perceived as very smart if she got a D in one of her four major subjects because she had been making out on a mountainside instead of memorizing the table of elements.

I got up, walked through the adjoining bathroom, and banged on Matt's door.

"Yeah?" He stuck his head into the bathroom, grinning when he saw it was me. "Want to take a study break?"

I couldn't help laughing at his exaggerated grin. But the laughter died when I thought of my chemistry teacher, Mr. Beal, passing out our exam papers with an evil gleam in his eyes.

"No, I'll have to pass tonight." I smiled back to let him know I *wished* I could take a break. "But do you think you could keep it down in here?"

As soon as I'd finished the sentence Nancy called up from the bottom of the stairs.

"Matt, you'll never guess who's here! Come downstairs!"

"Hang on a sec," Matt said to me. I noticed he had neglected to turn down the music. I went into his room and adjusted the volume myself.

When I stepped out into the hallway, Matt had already sprinted down the hall and to the landing. I followed him, curious to see who the Sunday night intruder could possibly be. I hadn't even heard the doorbell ring.

"Dave!" Matt took the rest of the stairs in one impressive leap. The guy at the bottom of the stairs was about six feet tall and tan, with sandy-colored, wavy hair and an athletic build. He and Matt exchanged high fives.

As I watched the apparent reunion from the hall I found myself frowning. I had been trying to have an important discussion with Matt, and he had sprinted off midsentence without a second thought. Did my problems mean nothing to him? I was glad his old friend had stopped by, sure, but that was no excuse for blatant rudeness. And how was I ever going to get any studying done with all this commotion in the house?

"You've got to meet Dina. She's really cool," I heard Matt say to this guy Dave, whoever he was.

Really cool? "Really cool" was how someone described the latest *Die Hard* movie or a sweater at Urban Outfitters. "Really cool" was not how one described the girl of his dreams. I was glad he'd mentioned me at all, but *please*.

I went back in my room and arranged myself at my desk. When I heard two sets of footsteps on the stairs, I waited tensely for Matt to knock on my door and introduce me to his friend. The knock didn't come.

What did return was the loud music, this time amplified by not one but two loud, off-key voices. I tried to concentrate, but the effort was futile. As I sat at my desk staring at my lab book the singing was replaced by the repeated thunk of a ball against the wall. Finally I slammed the book shut. I'd had enough.

Usually I liked the Grateful Dead. Now I was starting to wish I had never heard of them. I rose for the second time since I had sat down to work.

Without bothering to knock, I stuck my head through the bathroom door that opened into Matt's room. I wanted to conceal my irritation, but I wasn't sure it would be possible. "Matt?"

"Oh, hey!" Matt called. "Come in and meet Dave. I've known this guy forever. We went to camp together for five summers."

Dave stood and held out his hand with a friendly smile. "Nice to meet you, Dina. I couldn't believe it when my mom told me Matt was in Boston."

I ignored his hand. "Nice to meet you, Dave," I said, barely looking at him. At that point I didn't care if he played backgammon on the professional circuit or went shark hunting in Antarctica in his spare time.

With all the stress I was under to score well on this exam, I had reached my limit. "Matt, can I talk to you for a second? In private."

Matt gave me a funny look, but he got up. He shrugged at Dave and followed me through the bathroom and into my room.

"What exactly do you think you're doing?" I demanded.

"What do you mean, what am *I* doing?" he asked. "What are *you* doing, being so rude to my friend?"

I could hardly believe he was turning this on me. "Matt, don't you remember my exam? The one I've been stressed out about all weekend? The one I have to get a B on to make honors?" I gave him an incredulous look.

"Yes, I remember. But I'm not sure how my hanging out with Dave has any effect on your grades."

I was so fed up that I didn't even want to bother explaining. "Forget about it," I said. "I don't have the time. Just *be quiet.*" I hoped I hadn't yelled loudly enough to draw parental attention.

As I slammed the door in his face I heard him say one of my least favorite expressions. "Lighten up."

I kicked the door in anger, stubbing my toe in the process. I had forgotten that I was wearing soft slippers.

"What's her problem?" I heard Dave ask Matt through the door. I didn't stick around to hear the answer. I had too much to do.

It was after one o'clock in the morning when Dave finally left. I heard Matt walking him to the front door. Then I listened as Matt's footsteps pounded back up the stairs and down the hallway. They stopped right in front of my door. He knocked.

I thought about ignoring the insistent rap, but I had a few things to say to Matt myself. And now was as good a time as any. I certainly couldn't concentrate on my notes.

I got up from my desk, stretched, and walked to the door. When I opened it, Matt was yawning. He looked happy and relaxed. I was so tired, I could barely see straight.

It occurred to me that I was overreacting. That it wasn't Matt's fault I had saved all my studying until the last minute. And it wasn't his fault I had gone hiking all day.

I decided not to yell at him after all. He was so cute, I could forgive and forget this one time. Then he opened his mouth.

"Dina, I just wanted to wish you good luck on your test tomorrow." He looked pleased with himself, as though he was being especially thoughtful and considerate and deserved accolades for the effort. "And I understand why you were rude to Dave. Chemistry can be a real downer. That's why I always try to get my studying done in advance. Less stressful."

I couldn't believe his nerve! He was the one who had been loud and obnoxious for the last several hours. I had just been trying to study in peace. I was so taken aback that I couldn't think of an appropriately scathing response. Instead I slammed the door in his face. Again. Men!

* * *

"Okay, okay!" I said out loud as I fumbled for my alarm clock. It seemed as though I had shut my eyes just moments ago. I slammed the off button with my fist, and the clock stopped its obnoxious ringing.

I'll just take a fast shower to help me wake up. Then I'll get to school early.

Bleary-eyed, I stumbled out of bed, grabbed my robe from the hook on my closet door, and headed for the bathroom. But just as I was about to push open the door, the water started to run. Who would possibly be taking a shower at six o'clock in the morning? Who else? The person who shared my bathroom.

"Matt, is that you?" I banged on the door. I was in no mood for joking.

"Yeah!" he yelled back. "You've got to speak up, though. I'm in the shower." He sounded annoyingly cheerful. "What are you doing up so early?"

I seethed. It was easy enough for him to forget about our argument last night. He wasn't the one whose entire future rested on the hopes that Inga Webb would be studying at her usual carrel at the school library—ready and willing to share her last-minute expertise. He wasn't the one who had to do an advanced lab experiment, alone, in less than three hours. He wasn't the one who had to sit next to Denise Logsdon, the smartest girl in the school, and watch her finish her entire exam in half the scheduled time.

I bit my tongue so I wouldn't start screaming

about how his music and his idiotic friend had kept me up all night.

"Remember my final?" I answered shortly. He didn't respond. "Are you going to be a while?" I added.

"Shouldn't be too long." He'd heard *that*, obviously. "I'm playing morning soccer in the town summer league, and we start today. Dave told me about it. Awesome, huh?"

Although I could tell he was shouting from the strain in his voice, I could barely hear him over the shower. There was also a radio playing in the bathroom. I could hear one of the morning DJs announcing another sunny day in Boston.

Wait a second. Radio? I looked on the table beside my bed where my little portable radio usually sat. It wasn't there. It wasn't waterproof. I didn't remember being asked if it could be borrowed. Great.

When Matt finally emerged from the bathroom, I barely noticed that he was wearing only a towel. Well, okay. I totally noticed. But I didn't care.

"I'm out, Dina," he announced, standing in my doorway and shaking his head. Droplets of water fell onto my bed and bedside table.

Without a word I stormed past him into the bathroom. If I hurried, I could still catch Inga.

"All right, everybody! Two more laps of backstroke, and then we'll call it a day." Alison's unmistakable voice rang out across the pool area. I could hear her from the parking lot of the community center where Alison had worked for the past few summers.

Slamming my car door shut, I trudged miserably in the direction of the pool. As soon as I reached the clubhouse I could see Alison in her red tank suit. According to my calculations, she was finishing up a swim team practice right about now.

"Hey, Dina. Just give me five." She waved. She sounded and looked happy. I was jealous. After my day, and the exam from hell, I just felt tired.

She can afford to look happy, I thought. *She's not even taking chemistry. And she had her last final a week ago.*

Noticing that a few of my classmates were lurking around the Ping-Pong table, I decided to wait for Alison inside. I couldn't deal with any questions about my exam. I couldn't think about anything but Matt and chemistry. Chemistry and Matt. Chemistry *with* Matt. I was going crazy, and I needed a reality check. Enter Alison.

The smell of chlorine greeted me as I sat down on one of the old wooden benches by the deserted indoor pool. Alison and I had taken swimming lessons here when we were in elementary school.

I remembered my mom, waiting for our lessons to finish, sitting on these same benches. I ran my hand across the burnished wood.

Alison appeared from around the corner,

dripping wet. "Come on outside," she said. "We can still catch some late afternoon rays."

A couple of six- or seven-year-old girls ran by us, on their way to the locker room. Alison held out her hand to slap them five as they noticed her standing there.

"See you tomorrow, guys," she called. The girls looked thrilled by this off-duty interaction with their teacher.

If only I could be six years old again, I thought. *Then I wouldn't have to worry about getting into college. Or falling in love. Then I'd still have Mom.*

I followed Alison out to a grassy spot by the tennis courts. We collapsed on the lawn.

"What's up?" Alison asked, propping her chin in her hands. "You sounded kind of bummed on the phone."

"It's Matt," I began bluntly. "I'm not sure what to do."

"When can I meet this guy anyway?" Alison asked.

"Alison! Can we please stay on the subject for a change? I'm trying to tell you how Matt Harbison may have ruined my chance to make honors this semester."

Now Alison looked truly puzzled. "How did he manage to do that?" She sat up, curious, and then smacked her forehead with the palm of her hand. "Oh, my God! Your final! How did it go? Anna Freedenfeld told me it was incredibly, impossibly hard."

"It didn't go well," I said shortly. "And that's an understatement. Matt was up late with a friend, and they were so noisy that I couldn't get any work done, even after I asked him to be quiet. Twice." I remembered with a tiny twinge of guilt that in my panic about the exam I hadn't exactly asked nicely.

"Well, I wasn't there, so I can't say." Alison gave me a knowing look. "But it's not his fault that you didn't go to the study sessions Beal held earlier in the semester or stay in all weekend to prepare."

I was more than slightly annoyed that Alison was being so open-minded. Before I could tell Alison thanks but no thanks for her nonhelp, I noticed she was staring at me, her expression intent.

"What about the friend?" she asked.

"What do you mean?"

"The friend. Is he cute?"

"Alison, have you been listening to me at all? Even slightly?" I was exasperated.

There was more to life than cute guys, even if Alison didn't know it. Before she could answer me, a piercing whistle blew over by the pool.

"Phoenix?" A guy who looked like he was about nineteen was gesturing to Alison. "Your shift's on!"

"We'll talk later, Dina. I promise. But I've got to run." She jumped up and ran over to the guy with the whistle without so much as a backward glance. So much for the infallible advice of my boy-crazy best friend.

*   *   *

Dear Diary,

This has been one of the worst days of my entire life. And I've had some pretty bad days. Nancy and Dad seem tighter than ever, and Matt and I are barely on speaking terms—or rather, I'm barely on speaking terms with him, and he's too dense to know why. I have a horrible feeling I failed my chemistry final. And my best friend is so boy crazy she won't even listen to me when I have a serious problem.

I'm so glad school is over. Maybe I've been putting so much pressure on myself to get honors that I'm acting irrationally. It can't be possible that everyone in the world is suddenly out to get me. My dad, I guess, was justified when he yelled at me for taking off the other night. And I did overreact with Matt. In fact, I kind of flipped out. I can't believe I refused to shake Dave's hand like that.

I'm so confused, I could scream! Maybe a good night's sleep will help me put everything in perspective. Maybe, maybe not.

EIGHT

MATT

Dear Diary,

I DON'T KNOW what's going on with Dina. Everything seemed so great when we were hiking the other day. And of course there was that kiss. . . . But then that very same night she blows up at me because, get this, she thought my music was too loud. Even my mom's more mellow about the stereo. And when I turned it down—at her request, I might add—she came up with another list of complaints.

She actually thought Dave and I were laughing too much. Can you believe it? Maybe she was always this uptight, and I just didn't know it.

Okay. Sure. She had a final, and we all know that sucks. But couldn't she have brought her books down to the den if she couldn't deal with me and Dave hanging out in the next room? On the other hand, she did seem really stressed out. I don't know. Maybe I'm the one being selfish.

But wait. Maybe not. After she yells at me and embarrasses me in front of Dave, she has the nerve to get on my back again the very next morning. And why? Because I had the gall to get up early and, it gets better, to take a shower! How would I know that she was going to get up early too?

I don't know. Maybe Dina isn't the girl I thought she was. Maybe we should try to be friends—or even to tolerate each other—before we work on anything vaguely resembling a relationship. . . .

"Matt? Can I talk to you for a second?" Dina asked.

"Sure," I answered.

Dina looked great. She was wearing a Boston University T-shirt and bright blue running tights that matched her eyes. Her cheeks were pink, and she was just slightly out of breath.

She must just have come back from a jog, I noted. It was a perfect June morning, and I was sitting on the front steps reading *The Boston*

Globe. Up until this moment I had felt totally relaxed.

But having Dina so close made me tense. Even the sound of her voice made me nervous. I folded up the travel section and set it down beside me.

Dina and I had pretty much kept out of each other's way for the past couple of days. I figured she needed some time to cool off . . . and I wasn't that eager to snuggle up to her right away either. I still felt that she had overreacted and embarrassed me in front of my friend. But to say I was curious to hear what she had to say would be an understatement.

"You know my friend Alison?" Dina asked after a few moments of awkward silence. "The one you met this morning when she dropped off the book I'd left at her house?"

"Sure," I answered. "Why?"

For one horrible second I thought Dina was going to try to set me up with her best friend—to get me out of the way for good. Why had I acted so petty about her legitimate anger toward me? After all, I was the one who had been insensitive in the first place. *Everyone* complained that I took excessively long showers. And Dave and I *were* pretty noisy the other night.

Before I could formulate an appropriate apology, Dina spoke again. "Alison and I went for an early morning run together. When we got back to her house, she had a message on her machine."

She paused, and I nodded for her to continue. "One of the lifeguards at the community pool where she works broke his ankle this morning. He's out for two months, best-case scenario. They need a swim instructor for the rest of the summer. Interested?"

Interested? That was putting it mildly.

Far from pushing me away, Dina was actually hooking me up with a summer job. Maybe this was a good sign—a harbinger of things to come. And what a job! I had been a lifeguard before—man, what a tan! And I would still be able to play soccer in Dave's early morning league.

"The job sounds excellent," I told her. "Thanks for thinking of me." This seemed as good a time as any to try to make amends.

"It's not like I know any other jobless guys in the area who are CPR certified and have life-guarding experience." Dina didn't sound like she was all that interested in making conversation, let alone making amends.

Stupidly, instead of continuing to express my undying gratitude, I said the first thing that came into my mind. "How did you know I was CPR certified?" As soon as I said it I realized my mistake. The question sounded accusatory, as though I suspected Dina of running a credit check on me without my knowledge or of tracking down my FBI file—not that I had one.

"*You* told me," she said immediately. I could tell she was hurt. "In Colorado. You said you'd had to get your certificate to be a ski instructor."

The hurt in her voice changed to resentment halfway through her explanation. I decided against trying to make further headway. Better shut up now, or I would run the risk of doing even more damage with my big mouth.

"Well, anyway, thanks," I repeated, sheepishly this time. "When do I start?"

Without looking at me, Dina handed me a slip of paper with a phone number written on it.

"This is Alison's number. I told her you'd call her at work if you were interested. I've got to run. Later." She thrust the paper into my hand and ran into the house.

Leaving the newspaper on the steps, I followed her inside. I went into the kitchen and picked up the phone. Why wait? My summer needed a jump start in a major way.

"Hello, is Alison Phoenix available? It's about the lifeguard—" I started.

"Oh, are you the guy?" A stressed-out male voice cut off my formal introduction.

"Um, I don't know. I'm a guy, if that helps."

"And you're a comedian too. Just what we need around this place. No, seriously. She told me you'd be calling." He paused. "Can you come by the pool this afternoon?"

Short notice was my specialty.

"See you at noon?" I asked.

"Noon it is. Sounds great. Ask for Mike."

I hung up the phone. That was my kind of job

interview. No suit, no tie, no resumé. I'd have to make this up to Dina's friend somehow. And maybe even to Dina—if she'd let me.

"Mom, you want to watch the game with me? I'll make us some popcorn." My mom was washing dishes with Greg in the kitchen. They were standing shoulder to shoulder at the sink, laughing and joking around while she washed and he dried.

"Oh, I don't think so, hon," she answered. "Greg and I are going to try to catch a movie in town."

Great. I offer Red Sox–Yankees and a bowl of my special-recipe Harbison popcorn. He offers an overly air-conditioned theater, a B-rated flick, and hundreds of stir-crazy kids. Guess who wins—again? Zero points, Matt. Victory party for Greg.

I popped my popcorn anyway—enough for ten people, my mom would have said. But she had already gone upstairs to get ready by the time I'd finished making it. I poured myself a huge glass of soda and carried all my supplies into the den.

I settled down in the overstuffed, comfortable couch. If I had to spend the night solo, I could at least make sure I had all the proper amenities for a good time.

I had been following the Sox since way before my mom moved to Boston. A good game against the Yankees was as likely as anything else to make me stop thinking about my mom and Greg. I kept imagining them in the back row of the Cineplex. They were having fun while my dad was alone in a foreign city. *Dina would understand.*

What exactly was Dina up to tonight anyway? About an hour ago the phone had rung while we'd been eating dinner.

"Hello?" Dina had jumped up to answer it.

"I wonder who that could be?" Mr. Mazlin looked curious for a moment. Then he dug back into his lasagna. But *someone* was still curious. Me. As soon as she had identified the caller Dina had disappeared into the den. This was clearly a private call. What she didn't know was that the walls were thin. Mom and Mr. Mazlin were busy eating, so I strained to hear.

"Uh-huh. Okay. Wow. That's past my curfew." She giggled at something the caller said. "Really? That's so cute," she protested. "All right, then, I'll see you later tonight. I can't *wait.*" I winced.

When Dina returned to the table, she hadn't said a word. It was as if the phone had never rung. Her dad must have wanted to respect her privacy. He didn't pry. So I didn't either. What was certain was that she had run out the door as soon as the table was cleared. Maybe my mom knew where she'd gone.

"Mom?" I yelled up the stairs. There was no

answer. Great. She hadn't even said good-bye.

Suddenly I was sure that Dina had a boyfriend. She had been weird that morning when she'd told me about the job at the pool. She'd been out all day. And she dove for the telephone every time it rang. From the sound of the conversation she'd had at dinner, she had a date tonight! Not to mention the fact that she'd had her hair cut that morning in a new style and was wearing what I knew was her favorite pink T-shirt, her best jeans, and her cowboy boots. I didn't need much more proof.

The ringing sound of my mom's distinctive doorbell jarred me out of my funk. I stayed seated. Who was showing up on our doorstep at 8:30 P.M. on a Friday night? No one I needed to see. Not when I was imagining Dina in some nameless, faceless guy's arms. She didn't wear her cowboy boots when it was just the two of us hanging out. And she'd told me she saved them for special occasions. Like dates, probably.

The bell rang a few more times. Then the intruder started to rap on the door. Hard.

"Dina, are you there? It's me."

Wait a second. I knew that voice. That was the voice of one Alison Phoenix, my fairy godmother, the girl who had gotten me the job that could turn out to be my best summer employment yet.

I had spent the entire afternoon at the pool, and I'd had a great time. As soon as I arrived at the pool Mike had assigned me to tail Alison for the day to learn the ropes.

Alison was a blast. Funny, warm, and helpful, and the kids all loved her. I could see why Dina had picked her as a best friend. Maybe she could shed some light on where Dina was . . . and why she hadn't filled me in on her plans for the evening.

I jumped up, spilling popcorn all over the carpet in the process. I sprinted into the front hall and opened the door.

"Hi, Alison," I greeted her.

Alison looked surprised. She peered over my shoulder, as if to check whether or not I had been watching TV all alone. I was kind of embarrassed, but what could I do? If she thought I was a loser, it was too late now to conjure up a companion.

"Is Dina home?" she asked.

"No." I shook my head. "I don't know where she is." I tried to keep my voice from sounding bitter. "Our parents went to the movies, so I'm just catching the game. Sox versus the Yankees." I gestured to the television set. As Alison and I watched, the sportscaster came on to announce that the game was called on account of rain.

"Or maybe not." I grinned sheepishly. Alison smiled back.

"I wonder where Dina is," Alison murmured.

I shrugged. "Got me." This time I knew I sounded annoyed, but I couldn't help myself.

Alison glanced at her watch. "Hmmm. We were supposed to see a movie tonight. It's really unlike Dina to forget. If she gets home in the next few minutes, ask her to call me right away. Maybe she's just running late."

I breathed a sigh of relief. If Dina was going to spend the evening with Alison, then she probably didn't have a date after all. Maybe I had been a little paranoid when I had convinced myself that she was off making out with some guy. Or else the date was so hot that she'd even blown off her plans with Alison. The mere thought made me feel sick to my stomach.

I opened the door wider. "You can wait here if you want. I don't mind." It seemed rude to make her drive all the way home if she was just going to have to turn around and come back. Besides, I was feeling a little lonely. I wouldn't mind some company, even if it was for just a few minutes. I wasn't really flirting with Alison, I told myself. I was just being friendly. She'd gotten me a job, after all.

"You sure?" She looked hesitant, but she walked into the front hall.

"Definitely. Have a seat." I gestured to the living room couch, and we both started to laugh. Like the rug beneath it, the sofa was covered with popcorn.

We sat down, and Alison filled me in on the hot gossip about the pool staff. Mike, the head lifeguard, had just broken up with Pam, his ex-girlfriend, to go out with Ann, one of the tennis instructors. Mike and Ann were a perfect couple, Alison explained, so nobody felt too bad about Pam.

A perfect couple. Funny, that's what I'd thought Dina and I could be. But instead I'm sitting here listening to her best friend talk about people I don't even know.

"Alison, can I ask you something?" I blurted the words without thinking.

"Sure, Matt. Anything." She looked at me expectantly.

"Is Dina . . . seeing someone? That you know of?"

Alison looked taken aback. "Um, why do you ask?" She averted her eyes, avoiding mine.

"Just curious," I said, trying to make my voice sound casual.

"She likes to keep her options open," Alison said lightly, still avoiding eye contact. "But you should probably talk to Dina about that."

I looked at the clock on the living room wall. A lot of time had passed. And Dina still hadn't shown up. *And* on top of it all, her best friend was acting mighty suspicious about Dina's boyfriend status. Apparently I had been right after all. A great date was *exactly* the kind of thing that made a person forget they had made plans with their best friend.

Suddenly inspiration struck.

"Alison?" I said softly.

"Yeah?" She stood up, probably assuming I

106

was about to suggest she go home. It seemed fairly obvious that wherever Dina had gone, she wasn't coming back anytime soon.

"Is it too late to catch that movie?" I asked. Dina wasn't the only one who could go on dates.

"That was really fun." Alison sounded sincere, and I had to agree. I hadn't had such a good night out in a long time. The movie had been only so-so. But the rest of the evening was another story. We had run into a bunch of kids Alison knew from school in the lobby just before the movie had started. They had suggested a postmovie feast at the International House of Pancakes near Boston University.

The kids turned out to be really cool. Mia Heatherington and Caroline Suh were two of Dina and Alison's friends from school. Mia was quiet and kind of shy, but Caroline was outgoing enough for both of them. They were with their boyfriends, Alex Something-or-other-starting-with-a-B and Paul Cornelius. I had especially liked Paul, who was the varsity soccer captain at Brookline High. A girl named Kate Lowenstein and her boyfriend, Rob, had stopped by after the football game in Arlington, a nearby town. They'd been great—Kate was unbelievably funny. And Alison and I had gotten along surprisingly well, considering we'd just met that day. I already felt as though I'd known her for ages.

It had been kind of weird hanging out with all

these couples. I wondered if these guys thought Alison and I were a couple too. Nah. We were obviously just friends. Right?

Now we were back at the house, sitting in my mom's car. Suddenly, with no warning whatsoever, I yawned.

The digital clock in the car announced in neon blue that it was midnight.

"Pretty late," I commented.

"Yeah. I'd better be getting back." Alison put her arm across the back of the seat, making no movement toward either her backpack or the door. "I'm a little worried about Dina. It's not like her to go out without telling me where she's going."

"I'm sure she's fine," I said drily. *I'm sure she's just great.*

We sat there for a few minutes, enjoying the silence. I'd kept the car running so we could listen to the radio. The new Tracy Chapman song was playing.

"I love this song," Alison said.

"Yeah, me too."

Outside the car I heard a loud rustling in the blueberry bushes that bordered my mom's lawn. You had to go through the row of shrubbery to reach our front lawn from the neighbors' house. I'd realized that it was a shortcut on my first week in Boston. But who would be using it now? The night was so dark, I couldn't see anything, but the noise sounded louder than I'd expect from an animal. I turned on my brights.

Dina.

She looked exhausted. Her T-shirt was untucked from her jeans, and her hair was a mess. Only an idiot wouldn't know that she was sneaking back home after a hot date. With somebody else. Dina looked up, like the proverbial deer caught in headlights, and saw me. Then she saw Alison.

I felt a flash of guilt, for no real reason. Nothing had happened between me and Alison. We had just gone to a movie together—it hadn't been a date. So why did I suddenly feel a sense of impending disaster?

I looked over at Alison. She was staring through the windshield right at Dina. The tension in the car was practically tangible. For a moment no one moved.

"We haven't done anything wrong," I heard Alison whisper, almost to herself.

I was about to agree, but another look at Dina changed my mind. Why shouldn't I be out on a date with someone else? I was the one who had been sitting home alone while she had been off having a great time. I was so hurt and upset that I couldn't think clearly. I felt like my head was going to explode.

"Alison." I put my hand on her shoulder.

She turned slowly. I could tell she didn't want to look away from Dina. "Yeah?"

I'd been about to tell her that she needed to get out of the car, that I needed to be alone. But with one last glance at Dina, who was standing with her hands on her hips as though she had a right to be mad at me, I leaned across the front seat and kissed Alison full on the mouth. She didn't even have time to react.

She pushed me away. Immediately.

"Dina!" Alison yelled through the open window.

Dina didn't respond. Her eyes blazed, and even in the dark I could see that her face was white with fury.

Dina marched around to my side of the car. I had just kissed her best friend. Right in front of her. *What had I been thinking?* I opened my mouth, but no words came out. There was nothing to say.

Alison jumped out of the car and ran over to Dina, but when she tried to put an arm on Dina's shoulders, Dina roughly pushed her away.

"I don't care what you have to say!" she yelled at Alison, who had started to cry.

Dina stopped in front of my window, which I had rolled down. She bent down so our heads were at the same level. I held my breath.

"Matt Harbison and Alison Phoenix, I'd die perfectly happy if I never saw or spoke to either of you again," she said in a slow, steely voice.

Then Dina turned and ran into the house.

NINE

DINA

Dear Diary,

I HATE GUYS. I hate guys. I hate guys. I figure if I say it enough times, I might convince myself it's true.

Last night was the worst night of my entire life. I never thought I'd see the guy I love kissing my best friend—right in front of my face. I mean, this is like *Melrose Place* material! I wonder if a jury would consider the gruesome, bloody murder of Matt and Alison justifiable homicide?

Alison is supposed to be my best friend. Ha! She knew the whole story about Matt, and she still went out with him behind my back. Maybe she was mad that I had to baby-sit at the last minute, but it's not like she hasn't canceled on me tons of times. And for worse reasons than earning some extra cash. I thought it was enough that I left her, like, five messages apologizing. Apparently not.

And as for Matt, he's been trying to talk to me nonstop. He won't leave me alone. He keeps talking through my door about how it was all "a big mistake," that he was "just trying to make me jealous." He says he still loves me, and he wants to know where I was last night. Like I owe him an explanation! Ha! Whatever. I'm beginning to think you can't trust anyone anymore.

"This pasta is absolutely delicious, Greg." Nancy took a huge bite of the rapidly dwindling tangle of noodles on her plate.

I had to agree. When I had first heard that my dad was making dinner for the four of us, I had laughed. I had expected dinner to consist of one of two things—take-out food disguised as home-made or an inedible assortment of weird concoctions. Instead Dad served up genuine homemade pesto.

"This is really good, Mr. Mazlin." Matt was shoveling in his food so fast that he barely looked up from his plate. I was shocked to hear Matt's compliment. I didn't think I had ever heard Matt directly address my dad before, let alone praise him. Glancing back at Matt again, I felt my temperature rise. I couldn't stop thinking about how crushed I had been last night. Matt had tried to talk to me through my door for an hour or so, but I had put my head under my pillow and ignored him. After a while he gave up . . . and I had cried myself to sleep. He'd started up again in the morning, but I didn't want to hear what he had to say. Even if he was trying to make me jealous, what a lousy thing to do!

And Alison had called at least ten times since last night, but I hadn't taken a single one of her calls. What could she possibly have to say? As far as I was concerned, there was no valid excuse for their kiss. I tried to push to the back of my mind the fact that sure, I might have tried to make Matt think I had a date when I knew perfectly well I'd be playing computer games with Carl and Erica Houston all night. But that was no excuse for a kiss—I'd been pretending. Matt and Alison had betrayed me.

And who needed Matt and Alison anyway? I had other friends. And I would meet other guys. This wasn't the end of the world, after all.

It was unfortunate that my baby-sitting job had ended just when it did. And it was bad luck that my arrival home coincided perfectly with Matt and Alison's embrace.

But I was better off in the long run knowing what was what. Otherwise I could have gone on being a total fool all summer. And if Matt was going to be living in the house and sitting across from me at the dinner table, I would have to be polite. Or at least not homicidal.

But my dad and Nancy were practically oblivious to our presence at the dinner table. I was so grossed out by the way they were gazing into each other's eyes that I almost forgot Matt was a creep. Or I didn't forget, but for a moment I didn't care. I just wanted him to notice Dad and Nancy's latest public display of affection—he would understand exactly how I felt.

But when Matt finally looked up from his plate, he looked right at me. Not at our parents.

I nodded in the direction of Dad and Nancy. Matt's gaze went to his right, then down. My dad and his mom were holding hands.

I felt like a fourth-grader who thought kissing was disgusting, but the sight of their interlaced fingers made me sick. If my spacey but usually sane father was acting like the hero of a Harlequin romance in front of my very eyes, I didn't have to sit here and bear witness.

Cuddling on the couch was one thing; joking around while washing the dishes was another. But holding hands while they ate dinner? Give me a break.

The only thing that made me feel slightly better was the expression on Matt's face. We might have had our share of disagreements—to put it mildly—and I sure wasn't about to forgive him either for my chemistry final or whatever had gone on the night before with Alison. But there was one thing that we definitely had in common. And our mutual desire to break up our parents might just be enough to make me declare a temporary truce.

After dessert, which had included a homemade blueberry crumble so good it had nearly distracted me from my postmeal objective, I motioned for Matt to join me in the den. He looked understandably surprised—and hopeful. He probably thought I wanted to kiss and make up. Ha. He wasn't going to get off that easy.

Nancy, still exclaiming over the "absolutely scrumptious meal," had already offered to do the dishes. Of course my dad had immediately volunteered to help her.

I walked into the den. Matt followed.

"Dina, we need to talk," Matt said as soon as I closed the door behind us. The pleading look on his face almost softened my heart. But not quite.

"No, Matt. Don't even try it. I know I said I never wanted to speak to you again, but I've reconsidered. On one condition, and one condition only."

"Anything you want, anything at all. You have to know, I only—"

"Now is not the time for explanations," I interrupted in my most businesslike voice. "Now is the time for action."

Matt looked confused. "What kind of action?"

"I know we haven't been getting along," I went on, as though he hadn't spoken. "You know, first my final, then the shower. And then, worst of all, last night."

He tried to speak, but I cut him off again. "Obviously you think that because I happened to get an emergency baby-sitting job, it's a good idea to sneak around with my best friend. And to kiss her right in front of my face. Well, I disagree. I think it's disgusting."

I looked over to see how Matt was taking this unplanned speech. He looked dumbfounded. Good. Maybe he was starting to realize how badly he had hurt me.

"What did you just say?" he asked very slowly.

"You heard me," I snapped. "And quite frankly, I don't really care to discuss it anymore. You've tried to make your case, and I've decided not to forgive you. But I think we need to work together," I continued. "To join forces. Drastic circumstances call for drastic action." I looked at him for a reaction.

Matt might have broken my heart, and I might have lost him forever, but I wasn't about to give up my dad too. Not without a fight.

"*What* did you say you were doing last night?" Matt asked again.

Why could guys never focus on the point? I succumbed. "You know perfectly well what I was doing. I left so many messages on Alison's answering machine, I probably used up the entire tape. And your mom knew I was at the Houstons'. Don't pretend you didn't know I was taking care of two innocent kids while you were sliming around behind my back."

Matt looked truly stunned. Maybe he had thought I was going to forgive and forget overnight. Not a chance. But why did he have to look so cute? It made it hard to be angry.

I cleared my throat. "Anyway. Back to my plan."

"Are you talking about dinner tonight?" he asked.

I nodded. The stunned look on his face disappeared. It was replaced by an expression of disgust. "You're right about that. This has simply got to stop."

I was more than a little disappointed that he hadn't continued to protest my businesslike tone or my clear agenda. In spite of what I had told him, I'd half hoped he would take me in his arms and kiss me.

"I know," I said, trying to force the image of Matt and me kissing out of my mind. "My dad is acting totally irrationally. If he can't see how wrong this whole situation is, I'm going to have to take matters into my own hands. I figured you would feel the same way."

Matt sank into a chair. "It's obvious they're completely wrong for each other. You've never met my dad, but he's a great guy." Matt had a wistful look on his face.

I didn't point out that my dad was a pretty great guy too. I didn't want to start up an argument about which parent was more undeserving of the other.

"So what do you have in mind?" Matt's eyes were sparkling with excitement. He seemed just as ready to tackle this undesirable situation as I was.

"Two words," I said. "Operation Breakup."

"That's brilliant," Matt said, raising his hand to give me a high five.

I slapped his palm, feeling better than I had in the last twenty-four hours. If I had something to focus my energy on, maybe I would be able to forget about how miserable I was.

And spend some time with Matt, I admitted to myself. Although why I still wanted to be around the jerk was beyond me. At least I was sure about one thing. I was never going to forgive Alison. The role of best friend was sacred. Now that she had violated my trust, she deserved . . . what?

"I hope you don't mind if I also work on my secondary plan." Matt's voice broke into my satisfying daydream of Alison's head being impaled on a castle gate somewhere. So she'd been calling me night and day. And yeah, she'd written a letter and given it to my dad to give to me. I'd ripped it up and thrown it away. Too little, too late, as far as I was concerned.

"What's that?" I asked, holding my breath. Was there still hope for us after all? Maybe he was going to confess that his plan was to win me back if it was the last thing he did.

"Operation *Reunite*," he answered. "I want to get my parents back together."

I exhaled. *Oh, well. Who needs him anyway?*

Matt had a serious, faraway look in his eyes. "They're meant for each other. That's all there is to it. This could be the chance I've been waiting for."

I didn't answer. I was afraid I would start crying if I spoke.

"Well? Dina? Is that okay with you?"

"Sure, whatever you want," I said finally. "But let's keep our focus on the original plan. You can do whatever you want on your own time. But we're both going to have to give one hundred percent to Operation Breakup."

"Oh . . . there's one more thing," Matt added.

"What's that?" I asked.

Matt was staring at me intently. "I'll also spend the rest of the summer proving to you that what you saw last night wasn't what you *thought* you saw. Alison and I are just friends."

I didn't respond. Silently I prayed that somehow Matt *would* prove to me that nothing was going on between him and Alison. But seeing is believing—and last night I had seen him kiss my best friend.

"I can't tell you how much I've been looking forward to this." Nancy was literally beaming at me from the driver's seat. I felt sick to my stomach, but I managed to smile. I had to be pleasant, even if it felt like Chinese water torture.

"Me too," I said. "I love shopping on Newbury Street."

This shopping trip was all part of my grand plan. Realizing that I had a better chance of lying successfully to Nancy than to my dad, I had decided I needed to get her alone. If we ever found a parking spot, I could really do some damage.

And while Nancy and I were strolling around in the Back Bay neighborhood, Matt was going to be out in his mom's garden with my dad. Matt was teaching Dad everything he had always wanted to know about perennials but never had the chance to ask. In other words, he was torturing my dad by telling him fabricated horror stories about his mom while making him pull weeds at the same time.

"I wish I had more money to buy clothes for next fall. Almost everything I had was ruined in the hurricane." I tried to sound genuinely wistful. Nancy scanned the side street we were driving down for an open parking space.

"Are you short on cash?" Nancy sounded concerned. For just a moment I felt a twinge of guilt.

I looked over at her and noticed she was wearing the new red sweater my dad had brought home for her the night before. He had called the gift a "no reason" present. I didn't remember him ever just bringing home random "no rea-son" presents for my mom. The guilt faded fast.

"Yeah. I never have any money. And my dad doesn't understand that clothes are really impor-tant to a high-school girl. You know, the peer pressure . . ." My voice faded off suggestively. "It's just extra hard sometimes because all my friends and their parents feel sorry for me. Because of Mom. Sometimes Alison's mother even tries to take me shopping. But I hate it when people feel sorry for me."

"What?" Nancy sounded distracted. She was trying to parallel park in a tight spot next to a new BMW.

Bravely I persevered. "Yup. They all know why I never have any money or any new clothes."

"And why is that?" Nancy turned the wheel sharply to the left. The rear tire hit the curb, and the car lurched. But we were in. Nancy turned, still wearing her seat belt. She looked me square in the eye. "Dina, you know how much your dad loves you. He'll buy you some new clothes if you need them. I'm sure of it."

"Nancy, I know you know. We don't have to talk about it."

"You know I know *what?*" Now I had her. She was practically drooling. Time to move in for the kill.

"Well, when all Dad's money gets gambled away as soon as he makes it . . . there isn't much left over for jeans and sneakers."

"What!" Nancy was shocked. "What on earth are you talking about?"

I mustered up all my acting skills—what there were of them. I tried to look as though I had just put my foot in my mouth, big-time.

"Oh, no." Did I sound upset enough? "I just assumed he had told you. He usually tells *them* after a few days." This last line was a spontaneous stroke of genius.

"Them? Who's them?"

Had I gone too far? Nancy had a funny look on her face that I couldn't quite identify.

"Oh, nothing. I shouldn't have said anything. Forget about it."

"I think we better just stick to shopping, Dina." Nancy didn't look as though she had completely bought my story. But her tight-lipped expression and the lines between her eyes were a dead giveaway that I had hit some kind of nerve.

Once we were out of the car, I steered Nancy confidently into Emporio Armani, one of the most expensive stores in the city. The salespeople were so well dressed that it was intimidating. Stacks of sweaters in elegant colors lined the shelves. Evening gowns and immaculately tailored suits hung on the racks.

Immediately I tried to lose Nancy by an accessories display. I needed some time to plan my next strategy. Nancy, however, seemed to feel like chatting. She stuck to me like glue.

I can do chatting. I'm not so sure she'll like

hearing what I have to say. But I can chat with the best of them.

"So your dad has always liked the outdoors, right?" Nancy seemed entirely disinterested in the clothes. At least she had given me a perfect setup. I took a silk sweater off a shelf and held it up to myself in the mirror with a sad look at the price tag.

"What makes you say that?" I pretended to be shocked.

"Well, he's told me so himself. And he always seems more than willing to go on hikes or bike rides or do yard work."

I turned away so that she couldn't see my face. I removed a soft camel-hair blazer from a hanger.

"I think he knows that *you* like the outdoors. But more important, what do you think about this?"

Nancy glanced at the sweater. "Fine, fine. It's great." She turned her attention back to my face. "But Dina, what do you mean? Are you implying that Greg doesn't really like all of those activities?" Nancy sounded incredulous.

Bingo.

"I'm not *implying* anything. Let's not talk about it. I thought we were going to focus on the shopping."

I smiled. It was amazing what a little well-placed inflection could do.

Dear Diary,
   This afternoon went brilliantly. Even better than I had hoped. I dragged Nancy

123

to every store, boutique, chain, and mall in greater Boston. After about two hours my feet were killing me—and I was wearing sneakers. Nancy must have been dying in her pumps, but she never said a word.

And thanks to some expert guilt tripping and carefully placed pointed comments I manipulated Nancy into spending at least five hundred dollars on a lot of clothes I don't need. I didn't even want some of them!

By the time we reached the car—which had a parking ticket tucked under the windshield wiper (it must be my lucky day, for a change)—Nancy was exhausted. She was also in physical pain, in danger of imminent debt, and wondering what on earth she had gotten herself into. With me and my dad, who—sorry, Dad—I made sound like the lowest of the low.

When we finally got home, Nancy limped into the living room and collapsed onto the sofa. I ran upstairs to Matt's room, where we had agreed to meet at 4:00 P.M. From the huge grin on his face I could tell his day had gone as well as mine. He told me that he had basically convinced my dad that his mom was a shallow, superficial, spendthrift shopaholic. He told me a story that he seemed to find hilarious. Apparently he'd suggested that my dad plant some raspberry bushes smack in the middle of a patch of poison ivy. My dad could be kind of a hypochondriac, and Matt said he'd kept pointing to leaves and asking what they were. But when he'd started to pull up the poison ivy plants, Matt hadn't said a word. If my dad got poison ivy, even a mild case, the bad associations he'd have with Nancy's garden could save us a lot of stressful plotting. But poison ivy was pretty harsh. I hoped he wouldn't be too miserable.

Matt might have been exaggerating. But if he even planted a few seeds, he completed his part of the bargain. As for me, my work had been genius. Nancy won't just break up with my dad; she'll have him indicted.

When I told Matt how his mom had stopped to buy Band-Aids for her blisters, he looked concerned. But his face lit up as he described how my dad had called his chiropractor after the gardening stint because his back had felt so bad. And then he'd started to itch. . . .

Suddenly I didn't feel quite so gleeful. My dad's back tends to bother him only when he's under extreme stress. After my mom's funeral he was bedridden for a week.

As for working with Matt to break up our parents? I think it's going to be fine. I can barely remember how I used to feel about him—how soft his hair is, how brown and deep his eyes are. Oh, shut up! He's more interested in my best friend— and some best friend she turned out to be—than he is in me.

"Dad, are you busy at five-thirty?" I asked.

He looked frazzled, not to mention completely worn out from his strenuous morning in the garden with Matt.

"No. I'm free." He gave me a slightly suspicious look.

"How about a cup of coffee at Big Beans before my shift tonight? You can drive me, and I'll get a ride home."

"Sure." He still looked wary, but at least he had said yes. On to phase two. I would work on my dad this time. That left Nancy at home alone with Matt . . . where he could gauge whether or not I had made any headway this morning. I also hoped he would do some damage of his own.

An hour later Dad and I were seated at a corner booth in the back of Big Beans. The tables were farther apart here, and the noise level was on the low side. Dad ordered a couple of biscotti and a glass of lemonade. I opted for a strong cup of hot coffee, knowing I had a six-hour shift ahead of me. Plus the work I had to do on my dad.

I took a deep breath. It wasn't going to be easy to lie to my father. But sometimes a lie was for the other person's good. Alison told me that once when we were younger.

I had been scrupulously honest about our friend Katrina Holmberg's new haircut. "It won't grow back faster if she knows it's ugly," Alison had pointed out. This was even more extreme. I had to save my dad from himself.

I miss Alison, I realized suddenly. In spite of my ultraviolent revenge fantasies, it was hard not having my best friend around.

Alison hadn't quit calling me every hour on the hour. She had come over to the house twice, but I'd told my dad that I was sick and that I couldn't talk to her. He knew something was up but was clearly reluctant to pry. I couldn't figure out why Alison was being so persistent when she'd been caught red-handed like that. Was there something I was overlooking? I tried to imagine what Alison would say about Operation Breakup. I had a pretty good idea. I pushed it out of my mind.

"Dad," I plunged in, "there's something I've got to tell you . . . and you're not going to be happy about it."

My dad took a sip of his lemonade. "Hmmm. Needs more sugar." He added two more sugar packets to the glass. "Shoot."

"It's about Nancy. There's something you don't know."

My dad looked up at me. "Yes?" His voice gave nothing away.

"You know how she's been working at home in the mornings, when you've been at the office?"

Now my dad was starting to look mad. "Dina, I know perfectly well how you feel about my relationship with Nancy. But I don't have the time or the desire to hear you bad-mouth her. Whatever you're getting at, I suggest you just spit it out."

"She's been talking on the phone just about every day," I said slowly. "To Matt's dad."

My dad sputtered over a sip of his drink. He slammed his glass down on the table so hard, lemonade splashed out.

"I'm sorry, Dad."

He shook his head a couple of times. "Dina, are you telling me the truth?"

"I'm sorry, Dad," I repeated. "I thought you should know. But please don't tell her I told you. I don't want her to think I've been spying on her."

"I've got to go now. I'll see you at home." He picked up his keys and stormed out of Big Beans.

"Dina, are you still awake?"

I had been on the verge of falling asleep. Now I opened my eyes. Was I dreaming? There was another knock.

"Come in. I'm awake," I whispered back. The door creaked open.

"You've got to hear this," Matt hissed. "Follow me."

I got out of bed, pulled my robe over my shoulders, and followed Matt to the door of his mom's bedroom.

We pressed our ears against the door, straining to hear what was going on inside the room.

"They were louder before," Matt whispered in a barely audible voice. "They were yelling."

Suddenly I noticed that Matt was wearing really cute pajamas. And his hair was messy, as though he had just woken up. He looked great, and for a moment I could only concentrate on how close he was to me. The conversation in the bedroom seemed to fade away. But after a few seconds I forced myself to shift my attention away from Matt.

Inside the room there was silence. Apparently whatever discussion Matt had been eavesdropping on had ended.

Both of us almost jumped through the ceiling when the door sprang open. Dad appeared, his pillow and a blanket in his arms.

Obviously he was absorbed in whatever he was thinking. He didn't even notice Matt and me standing guiltily in the hallway. At least he didn't acknowledge us. He simply stomped down the hall and headed down the stairs. He must have been planning to sleep on the couch.

Matt and I exchanged a look. We tiptoed silently back to our rooms.

"Good night," I whispered when we reached Matt's bedroom door. "We'll talk tomorrow."

Matt gave me a thumbs-up sign before he disappeared into his dark room.

Inside my own room I flopped onto my bed. Life was so complicated. Why did I feel so depressed, thinking about my dad all alone downstairs? Wasn't that exactly what I wanted? And if I hated Matt so much, why did I feel dizzy every time he got within ten feet of me?

I looked at the phone over on my desk. Sitting up in bed, I looked at my digital clock. It was too late to make phone calls, but I needed to talk to Alison. Then I sighed, remembering that I wasn't speaking to her.

I got up and went into the bathroom to brush my teeth and get a glass of water. When I opened the door, I blinked. Was this the same bathroom that had been a pit ever since Matt had arrived at the house? The floor had been scrubbed. My pink towels were neatly folded and hung on the rack, just the way I liked them. My toothbrush was by the sink, and a piece of paper had been rolled around it and fastened with a rubber band. A 100 Grand candy bar sat next to it. Huh?

I took off the rubber band and unrolled the sheet of paper.

Dina—Please listen to me. You misinterpreted what you saw. I was just trying to make you jealous. I thought you'd gone out with somebody else. I love you. Matt.

For just a moment I softened. Matt had remembered my favorite candy bar. And he'd actually cleaned the bathroom after I'd complained for days to no avail.

But facts were facts. He'd kissed another girl. Right in front of me. I wasn't going to bow down just because of a stupid candy bar. I started to storm out of the bathroom. At the last minute I turned back and grabbed the candy.

Back in my room I slipped back under the covers and settled in for yet another sleepless night. I couldn't lie to myself—I missed my best friend.

Finally I got out of bed again and got the cordless phone off my desk. I brought it back into bed with me. Just then the phone rang. I answered it immediately so it wouldn't wake anyone else up.

"Al?" I said.

"How'd you know?"

"Lucky guess," I answered. "Plus the fact that you've called about a zillion times since yesterday and you're driving everyone here nuts."

Alison laughed.

"If you're still willing to talk, I'm willing to

131

listen," I said. "So let's hear it. Talk." I unwrapped the candy bar and took a big bite.

"Well, first of all, I didn't even get your messages until the next morning. My little brother had turned the volume off on the phone *and* the answering machine. I had no idea you were babysitting. I thought you'd forgotten that we were supposed to hang out."

Alison took a deep breath. I waited for her to continue.

"And second of all, if you'd stop to think for one measly minute, you'd realize that all I wanted was for you and Matt to be together. I even tried to make you seem mysterious and alluring by hinting that you were a rabid dater. I guess that backfired."

I considered this. "So there's nothing between you and Matt?" I was starting to feel a bit foolish for having doubted Alison in the first place. She didn't have it in her to betray me like that.

"If you can't see it, then you're blind. Matt was trying to make you jealous. He doesn't know anyone else is even alive." We were both silent for a second. I took another bite of chocolate.

"And one last thing." Alison sounded deadly serious.

"Yeah?"

"What's that you're eating anyway? It sounds like you're chomping on gravel."

I sighed. I was still furious at Matt. But at least I had my best friend back.

TEN

MATT

"THINK FAST!" I tossed a cold diet Coke to Alison. I headed over to the patch of grass by the pool where she was sitting in a lounge chair, sunbathing during her break. Fortunately she'd forgiven me when I'd called to apologize for my horrendous behavior. Alison had said she'd understood, that she got crazy jealous sometimes too.

"Hey, Matt. Thanks." She held up the can in a mock toast. "To breaks." After a long gulp she looked over at me.

I had sat down on the adjoining lounge chair. I held my own unopened Coke up to my forehead. The cold aluminum felt good against my hot skin.

Unfortunately it wasn't just the weather that was making me feel overheated. Every time I thought about Dina, I felt so confused and conflicted and lovesick that I thought my head would burst. I still couldn't believe she had been baby-sitting Carl and Erica when I thought she had been sneaking around with some guy. And I couldn't believe I had been such an idiot.

"Everything okay?" Alison sounded concerned.

Were my feelings so painfully obvious? At this point I didn't even care. What did I have to lose anyway? Maybe Dina's best friend would be able to help me out.

"Yeah, I guess so. I'm okay." I knew I didn't sound convincing. Not that I was trying all that hard.

I wanted Alison's advice. But was it too soon after our disastrous kiss to talk to Alison about Dina? I knew that she and Dina had made up, but had Alison explained the story from my perspective at all? Had she tried to tell Dina that I'd been a fool in a fit of jealousy? That I'd kissed her only to make Dina angry?

Doubtful. Or at least it was doubtful that Dina would even listen to her. She hadn't been swayed by any of my desperate efforts thus far. But Alison was my only hope. If anyone could convince Dina to give me another chance, it was her.

I knew that Alison had gone on a date with Jason Stawnychy, the tennis pro at the pool, and that she was really into him. I had heard from several of the other swim instructors that he'd had a crush on her for forever. All I felt for Alison was friendship. I was positive she felt the same way about me.

And I was way over my head with Dina. I loved her, but she didn't know it. And I didn't know how she felt about me. Not to mention the fact that only days after it had begun, Operation Breakup was already bringing out both of our worst sides. I had felt sick the other night when we actually got Dina's dad to sleep on the living room couch.

Did I really want to drag Dina's best friend any further into this mess . . . because of me?

"Is it Dina?" Alison set her soda down on the concrete and took off her cat-eye sunglasses.

That was all the encouragement I needed. I slunk farther down into the chair until I was practically prone. Kind of like how people always lie down on couches in psychiatrists' offices in the movies. At least this was free.

"Yeah, it's Dina," I admitted. "I don't know if she told you . . ."

"Told me what?" Alison asked.

"We've sort of been, well, trying to break up our parents." The horrified expression on Alison's face let me know that she didn't approve of Operation Breakup. I felt like a jerk. I wanted to tell Alison that I had agreed to Dina's plan so quickly partly because it would mean spending time with Dina. And I wondered if Dina had designed the scheme partly for the same reason.

Already I was regretting the fact that we had taken our parents' lives into our own hands. Not that I suddenly loved Greg Mazlin or anything, but my mom's business was her own. I couldn't believe I'd never seen that so clearly before.

This morning, when I saw the circles under my mom's eyes, I had started to think about what I was really doing. My mom loved me so much. Did I really want to be the source of her misery?

"You're kidding me." Alison looked genuinely appalled. "Why would you do that?"

But before I could explain, she tapped her forehead with her index finger. "I get it. Dina doesn't want anyone to replace her mom. And you feel protective about your dad. You probably even want your mom and dad to get back together. In fact, that's probably part of the reason you're here in Boston in the first place."

I was beginning to see exactly what Dina saw in Alison. She was pretty perceptive. I wondered if she had any idea how much I still cared about her best friend.

"That's amazing. You're totally right. Even the part about why I'm here in Boston. I told myself that I just wanted to spend some time with my mom. And while that's definitely true, it's not the whole truth."

Alison nodded. "You know, everyone wants their parents to be together. It's totally normal. But unless yours are different from everybody else's, they probably weren't happy together. And you can't fix that, no matter what you do."

I sighed. "Yeah. I'm beginning to think you're right. I came here this summer with an agenda. But I'm beginning to see the holes in the plan." I took a deep breath.

Wasn't admitting that I had a problem the first step to recovery?

"My parents are more likely to take up skydiving than they are to remarry each other," I confessed to Alison. "They fought all the time when they were together. Now I really just want them both to be okay."

Alison smiled. "Take that one step further. Why shouldn't you want for your parents everything you want for yourself? Don't you think they deserve to be really, truly happy? Don't you think you deserve the same thing?" She gave me a pointed look.

I knew what she was talking about.

And I knew she knew that I loved Dina.

"Thanks, Alison. You're a real friend."

I meant it. In a very short time we had already been through a lot together. I had come to respect Alison not just as Dina's friend but as my own. But this was not the time for lengthy proclamations of gratitude.

Alison looked at her watch and jumped up off the lounge chair. "I've got swim team in five minutes," she explained. "Can't be late. I know you'll do the right thing, though. Let me know what happens."

Maybe I could convince Dina to forgive me after all. But I couldn't do it at the pool.

"Hey, Al?" I called out to her as she jogged off.

"Yeah?" She stopped and turned around.

"Say hi to Jason for me!"

Even from a distance I could tell she was blushing. Good. Everything was okay between *us* anyway.

I looked out at the calm, reflective surface of the pool. In just minutes the water would be full of screaming kids and yelling instructors. For now it was as still as the sky. I got up with new-found resolve.

There was someone else with whom I needed to share my revelations. Someone important.

I just hoped it wasn't too late to make Dina understand what I was feeling.

The traffic was bumper to bumper all the way to Big Beans. I turned the radio up to top volume to distract myself. An Alanis Morissette song came on that had been number one on the pop charts when Dina and I had met in Colorado.

I could remember exactly how she had looked in her ice blue ski jacket, her cheeks bright red from the wind. We had just come in for a hot chocolate break, and this song had been blasting from someone's boom box. "I love her voice," Dina had said. I had agreed. But now I couldn't stand to be reminded of those times. I changed the station.

When the DJ announced that the afternoon's theme was "The Summer of Love," I switched the station again to one that played classical music only. No words—it would be less dangerous.

Finally, after half an hour, I made it to the coffee bar. I was ready to talk. But I couldn't find an empty space. For ten more minutes I drove around and around the block. I passed a couple of handicapped spaces on Massachusetts Avenue and considered parking illegally. I must have hit every red light in the area. As I sat in traffic I tried to plan out what I wanted to say to Dina. "I love you" was the first thing that came to mind. But I didn't want to freak her out. I had some explaining to do first.

Finally I saw a red Jeep Cherokee pulling out of the farthest corner of the parking lot in front of Big Beans. I sped into the spot. I was so impatient to talk to Dina, I probably would have punched my fist through the window if someone else had beaten me to the space.

As I walked toward the Big Beans entrance I felt more and more nervous. By the time I reached the doorway, I was practically shaking.

Instead of going right in, I stood to the left of the doorway, where I could peek in at Dina through the big front window without being seen.

The place was packed. All the tables were taken. The two guys and girl behind the counter serving takeout looked frantic. I scanned the crowded room. There she was—the girl of my dreams. She was serving a plate of cookies to a guy doing a crossword puzzle.

Dina looked beautiful, even in her Big Beans apron. Her hair was tied back in a neat, professional ponytail. Like the employees behind the counter, she looked stressed out.

A couple about my age gave me a strange look as they walked past me into the coffee bar. I wasn't the slightest bit embarrassed to be so blatantly spying. I just wished I could get a better view.

Just then a guy appeared in my line of vision. Not too tall, dark hair, glasses, athletic build. He was wearing an apron identical to Dina's.

He must be a fellow waiter, I thought. *It looks like they know each other pretty well.*

As I watched, leaning so close to the glass that my nose was practically touching it, the guy leaned close to Dina. He whispered something in her ear. She laughed and punched him lightly on the arm.

I wished desperately that I could hear what they were saying. From where I stood, it looked like they were flirting.

Another couple walking into the shop gave me a suspicious glance. The man whispered something to the woman, who looked back over her shoulder at me. But at this point the last thing I cared about was how I appeared to a bunch of strangers.

All I cared about was Dina.

I punched the glass of the big window I was leaning on so hard I hurt my hand. Not only did it appear that I wasn't exactly on the route to winning Dina back, it seemed that I was about to lose her to somebody else. Somebody handsome and apparently pretty funny. A guy who had the advantage of working beside her every day.

For a moment I thought Dina was looking right at me. I jumped back, out of her line of vision. Had she seen me? It was hard to say. But there was no reason whatsoever for me to stick around.

I turned and jogged back to my car. Gunning the engine, I ripped out of the lot. As I turned the corner to pull out onto the street, I heard someone calling my name.

"Matt! Wait! Let me explain!" It was Dina. She had run right out of Big Beans with her apron on, and she was standing on the sidewalk, waving to me.

I glanced in the rearview mirror but kept driving. Who needed to have it explained in person that he was being made a fool of?

Not Matt Harbison.

Dear Diary,

I feel like a complete and utter idiot. I thought I was getting encouragement from Alison to make up with Dina. And in spite of everything that's happened, Alison is still Dina's best friend in the world. You'd think she would know Dina better than anyone else.

But when I showed up at her job, ready to apologize, she was flirting with another guy! I guess she's not exactly cheating on me. It's not as though we have any kind of a commitment, let alone an understanding. But how can she think of being with anyone but me? How could she refuse to let me explain my own behavior and then do the same thing to me by flirting with another guy right there in Big Beans, in front of the whole town?

I think we need to stop interfering in our parents' relationship (I can hardly believe I'm saying it, but I do). But I don't feel like talking about that—or anything else—with Dina right now.

I guess it's not going to be easy to avoid her for long. I mean, she does live in the same house. . . .

ELEVEN

DINA

Dear Diary,

I THINK MY plan today may have back-fired. I was bringing a couple of tall lattés to a couple sitting at a window table when I saw Matt's car pull into the parking lot. I couldn't imagine what he was doing there, but you'd better believe I was curious. Five minutes passed, then ten. No Matt. It wouldn't take ten minutes to walk backward on your hands through our parking lot. I was pretty sure Matt wasn't going into Caitlin's Corner, the only other store in our strip.

Then I caught a glimpse of Matt's red jacket just outside the door. A few seconds later I turned quickly and saw him actually peering in the window, watching me.

For some reason I panicked. I couldn't imagine what he was doing there. And I was mad. Who did he think he was following me to work like some kind of spy? So what do I do? I start flirting with Joel, who I've known since I was practically in diapers and who's basically engaged to Sandra Merriam.

In retrospect, I guess I was fantasizing that Matt would storm in, tell off Joel, and proclaim his undying love for me. I don't know why I always have these stupid, melodramatic, hyperromantic ideas.

So how did Matt react? The way any sane person would in a similar situation. I hate to say it, but the way I reacted . . . he took off. He wouldn't listen to me. He still won't. And I can't say that I blame him. It's funny looking at this from the other side.

Also, Operation Breakup is really getting me down. I keep picturing my mom giving me her most disappointed look—the one she reserved for those times when I had really, unequivocally let her down. Can it be that I've been horribly wrong about what was best for my dad? For me? When my dad was with Nancy and everything was great, he was happier than he had been in years. I can't deny that.

When they aren't getting along, like now, he gets this sad look that would bring tears to the Mona Lisa.

And then there's Matt. If I back out of Operation Breakup now, we would have no reason to spend so much time together. I mean, part of the reason I enlisted him in the plan was so we could hang out, maybe begin to make amends. If I quit, where would we stand?

Why, why, why is it so hard to be sixteen?

Brookline is a beautiful town, I thought for maybe the thousandth time in my life as I pedaled by the well-kept public tennis courts and picturesque softball field I had played on as a little girl.

I always went on a bike ride when I needed to think. I had never had a problem quite like this one, so I was prepared to ride around all day if that's how long it took for anything to make sense.

A bunch of kids were getting ready for softball practice out on the field. I stopped my bike, leaned it up against a tree, and sat down to watch for a few minutes. Although the Matt and Alison encounter was still fresh enough to be sharply painful, I forced myself to review in my mind what had happened the other night.

When Mrs. Houston had called and told me that Carl and Erica's grandmother was sick and that she needed a sitter at the last minute, I hadn't thought twice. Ever since my mom died, I've been especially sensitive to people dealing with illness. And I had loved baby-sitting for the Houston twins for years.

I called Alison to let her know, but the machine picked up. It was unusual for no one to be home at the Phoenix house, so I called back a bunch of times. No answer. I now knew why. Her annoying little brother was always messing around with the phone. I couldn't believe it hadn't occurred to me myself before Alison had clued me in.

But the kiss had hurt me, more than Matt could possibly know. I'd thought he was in love with me, after all.

I couldn't really be surprised by Matt's reaction to my flirting with Joel. He felt exactly the same way I did, I was sure of it. In some ways Matt and I were so alike. That was part of the reason I felt deep down inside that we were meant for each other. How had we gotten ourselves in so much trouble? I thought true love was supposed to be easy.

Down on the softball field the kids had organized themselves into teams. Now they were arranging themselves on the field. I got up and climbed onto my bike. Clearly I wasn't ready to go home yet. But I couldn't just sit here replaying the same scene in my mind over and over again either.

I rode through my favorite residential

neighborhoods. Then I went by our old apartment to check on the construction. From the sidewalk everything looked the same. I could tell from the trucks parked on the curb that work was going on inside. But there were no clues as to the estimated time of completion.

Then I rode by Boston University and checked to see if my dad's car was parked outside his office. It wasn't, so I kept going. At the red light just past campus I stopped, glad for a moment to catch my breath. I'd been on the road for a long time.

A couple was crossing the street. They were a few years older than me, maybe college age. The girl was tall and blond. From where I stood perched on my bike, she looked kind of like me. The guy had dark wavy hair. He looked like . . . Matt.

When the light turned, I didn't even notice it. I just stood there, not even really noticing the tears that were filling my eyes.

I need to be with Matt. I need to make him understand and to listen to his explanation. If I hurry, I can catch him at the pool.

Before the light had a chance to turn red again, I took off.

"Hey, Dina! What's up?" James Engel, a guy from my homeroom, waved at me as he got into his car. His red hair gleamed in the bright afternoon sun.

"Not much!" I called back. I had no time for

147

making conversation with random guys. I practically threw my bike at the bike rack and took a deep breath.

Through the trees I could see a bunch of kids hanging around by the diving board. Lessons were still in session—I wasn't too late.

I locked up my bike and jogged to the outdoor pool and tennis courts. Scanning the expanse, I saw not Matt but Alison.

She was standing by the tennis courts, talking to Jason, the tennis pro who was varsity captain at Brookline High during the school year. I couldn't hear their conversation from where I was standing. But Alison looked great in her cutoffs and red regulation tank suit. She looked happy.

From the looks of their body language there was more than just friendship between them. I smiled. They made a great-looking couple.

As I stood staring at her, Alison caught sight of me. In a flash she dropped the towel and the bag she was holding, leaving Jason midsentence.

"Dina!" she called as she ran. "You've got to find Matt," she said, out of breath from her run. "He's dying to talk to you."

"Not as much as I want to talk to him," I said. I could barely keep from crying. My life was beginning to seem like a series of misunderstandings.

"Dina, you have to believe me. I've been telling you all along. There has never been, is not, and never will be anything between me and Matt. That kiss was a mistake. Matt regretted it the second after it happened. Like I've told you a million times, he thought you were sneaking around behind his back." She sounded convincing, but I had to be sure.

"Alison? Can I ask you something?"

She squeezed my shoulder, and my sobs subsided. "Of course. Anything."

"Do you think I still have a chance with Matt? He saw me flirting with Joel today at work, and I could tell he was really mad . . . not to mention the fact that there are like a dozen gorgeous girls who work at the pool. He kissed you—maybe he's kissed someone else too."

In the background kids were laughing and splashing in the pool. A tennis match was being fought out on the court where Alison had stood moments before. But all I could focus on was Alison's face.

"Dina, you have to listen to me. There is nothing between me and Matt Harbison. And there's nothing between Matt and any girl who works at the pool. Because he's in love with somebody else."

My heart plummeted. Not only did Matt love somebody else, he had confided in Alison. Maybe that's why he had shown up at Big Beans. He had intended to break the news to me, but he had chickened out at the last minute. Maybe he hadn't seen me flirting with Joel after all. Maybe he was just scared to face me.

I didn't want to know who the girl was . . . I

could barely bring myself to ask. But I had no real choice. I would go crazy if I didn't know who he was in love with.

"Who?" I whispered. "Who is Matt in love with?"

Alison looked puzzled for a moment. Then she smiled. She hugged me again, laughing. "He's in love with you, you clueless moron. He told me so himself."

She shook me. I smiled weakly, unsure what to believe. But I was incredibly relieved that Alison hadn't confirmed my worst fears.

"Hasn't he told you?" she asked.

"He hasn't exactly had a chance," I answered slowly. I had a flashback to the scene at Big Beans. It must have looked horrible to Matt. Me and Joel flirting like crazy right there in front of everyone. Alison looked confused.

"Do you have time to get a burger some-where?" I asked. "This may be more complicated than I thought."

"I'll have those fries extra well-done," Alison told the waitress.

I sighed indulgently. Like the Meg Ryan char-acter in *When Harry Met Sally,* Alison always asked for her food done in a particular way. She never just ordered off the menu. Sometimes her habit annoyed me because it meant we had to wait extra long for our food. But right now I was so happy to be sitting with her in our favorite booth at Harry's Burgers that I wouldn't have cared if she asked for each of the fries to be cooked individually.

The waitress left, and Alison plunged right in. "You want to talk about your parents, right? Matt filled me in on what's been going on."

"Yeah. It's pretty bad," I admitted. "Did he tell you about Operation Breakup?"

"In so many words," Alison said. "Bad idea, huh?"

"I guess so. I mean, it seemed like such a good plan at the time. We both wanted the same thing. To break them up. In retrospect I think it's just making us both act like jerks."

Alison nodded. "Sounds like it to me." She paused, choosing her words carefully. "Remember when your mom took us to Plum Island a few years ago, just before she got sick again?"

I remembered. How could I forget? That was the last perfect day Mom and I had had together. The following day my mom had gone in for a biopsy and learned that the cancer was back. I nodded.

"Well, I know this is going to sound crazy, but I think your mom knew," Alison said softly. "That she was sick again, I mean."

"What are you talking about? How could she have known?"

"During lunch, at that clam shack right on the beach, you got up to go to the bathroom. While you were gone, your mom got kind of quiet.

151

When I asked her if she was feeling all right, she smiled and said she was fine. But then she leaned close to me. 'Make sure they take care of each other, Alison,' she whispered."

I was so transfixed by Alison's story that I didn't even notice when the waitress set my milk shake down in front of me. "And then?"

Alison continued. " 'But don't let Dina get too protective of her dad,' she told me. 'He'll be okay. He knows how much I loved him.' " Alison had tears in her eyes as she finished the story.

I just stared at her, spellbound by what I was hearing. "Are you sure?" I whispered.

"Perfectly sure. I remember especially that she said "loved him." I thought it was weird that she used the past tense. But I just nodded and promised not to tell you what she had said. And until now I never did."

Harry's Burgers had never seemed like such a special place before. Even the decrepit red leatherette of the booths and the ugly neon pink aprons the waitresses were forced to wear seemed especially poignant. I knew one thing—I would never forget this moment.

I had no words to express what I was feeling. I was overcome—with love for my mom and regret for the brevity of her life. Incredible warmth at the thought of the love she had shared with my dad. Appreciation of her wisdom and selflessness.

There was no doubt about it. In spite of

everything we had been through, Alison was the best friend a girl could ever have.

Dear Diary,

I've got to crash—I'm exhausted. But I wanted to get this down while it's fresh in my mind. Two entries in one day—you know it's important.

First of all, I had a once-in-a-lifetime conversation with Alison today. I'm going to think about what she said and whether or not I think she's out of her mind. Matt doesn't act like he cares. But at least I know what I have to do about my dad. It was really powerful hearing that story about my mom. For the first time in a long time I felt as though she was still a part of my life. Almost like she was watching over me or something.

The second big thing is this: Matt and I decided we're going to fix a gourmet meal for our parents tomorrow night and come clean about Operation Breakup. He wasn't exactly friendly when he brought up the idea. But at least he's speaking to me.

Although I would never tell him so, I'm thrilled to have a reason to spend time with him, just the two of us. Maybe in between discussions about how to undo the damage we may have done to our parents' relationship, we can talk about what we're going to do with our own.

TWELVE

MATT

"TOMATO PASTE, OREGANO, extra-virgin olive oil . . ." Dina's voice trailed off as she checked items off the grocery list we had made earlier.

We were in Super Shop, the biggest and best grocery store in Brookline, wandering the aisles in what had to be the most disorganized search for ingredients in the history of shopping.

"Are you sure this is a good idea?" Dina stopped short with the half-full cart she was pushing.

I was scanning the shelves for the brand of angel-hair pasta my mom always bought.

"What do you mean, a good idea? I think it's the only good idea either one of us has had in quite some time."

She nodded. "Good point."

Somewhere in the produce section the tension that had been building between me and Dina since the moment we had first laid eyes on each other here in Boston had broken. Or started to break anyway. I felt perfectly normal grocery shopping with her. Better than normal. Great.

It seemed that we had both decided to really make an all-out effort to put our differences aside for the time being.

For one thing, there was definitely something going on with our parents. And it didn't look good. For the past couple of nights Dina's dad had slept on the living room couch. He and my mom had barely spoken, even when we were around to watch them. We had killed Operation Breakup, but whatever we had said and done had already had its effects.

Dina took the pasta I'd finally located from me and placed it in the cart. "This just seems too easy somehow. Like one dinner will make up for how insensitive we've been."

"I don't think we really have any choice," I said. It was hard for me to believe that I'd ever thought Operation Breakup was a good idea.

I was beginning to understand the situation from Dina's perspective, though. I had spent a lot of time over the last few days trying to imagine what it would be like to lose either my mom or my dad. Even my lame attempts at imagining one of them dying left me shaken and upset. It must have been incomprehensible for her to lose a parent at such an age—young enough to desperately need her mother, old enough to really miss her once she was gone.

Trying to see our parents' relationship from Dina's point of view had made me come full circle. I had rethought my own attitude too—about my own situation, that is.

My parents both loved me; there had never been any doubt about that. I thought of all my friends with divorced parents who had decided it would be easier to cut their kids out of their lives than to interact with their ex-spouse. Some of my friends hadn't seen one of their parents in years. I finally realized that I couldn't save my parents' marriage. But I was lucky to have them both in my life.

Dina was pushing the cart. Apparently while I'd been lost in thought, she had been doing some thinking of her own. Suddenly she started to laugh. She laughed so hard, she leaned against a glass door, holding her side.

I just stood there watching her, making apologetic faces to customers who walked by and stared.

Finally she was able to speak, albeit through alternate fits of giggling. "Do you really think your mom believed all that stuff about my dad's gambling habit?"

I started to laugh too. Some of the stories we had come up with had been truly far-fetched.

"What about my mom's supposed shopaholic problem?" The thought of my down-to-earth, outdoorsy mom on a credit card binge in Emporio Armani set me off again.

By this point we were both red-faced and hysterical.

"What about me telling your mom that my dad thinks women should stay in the kitchen where they belong?" Dina said. "My mom would turn over in her grave!"

"They must think we're insane. Maybe that's what's causing them to fight—they can't decide which of them has the most imbalanced teenager."

Another round of laughter.

"My rib cage hurts," Dina said finally. We leaned on our cart for support. I was out of breath.

"Mine too," I said.

But it was a good kind of pain. A lot better than heartache, I'll tell you that much.

When we pulled into the driveway an hour later, we were still laughing. I hadn't felt so close to Dina in a long time. I could tell she felt the exact same way. Even the silences we had shared had been companionable ones. I was almost afraid to hope that any of it meant anything. It seemed as though every time I thought things might be getting better, trouble ensued.

With two heavy bags of groceries in each of our arms we walked side by side up the path to the kitchen door. I put one of my bags down on the patio to unlock the door. I could hear voices in the kitchen.

"They're not supposed to be here yet," I whispered to Dina. She shrugged.

"What are we going to do? We have to go in. The food will go bad."

"True," she agreed.

I unlocked the door, picked up my other bag, and pushed the door open with my foot.

My mom was standing by the sink. Her face was blotchy and her eyes were swollen, as though she had been crying.

Greg was seated at the kitchen table, staring off into space. I glanced back at Dina. She looked worried, big-time. Something was going on here. And I had the sense it wasn't something good.

"Hi, you guys," Dina said tentatively.

Silence. Dead silence.

"Um, are you guys hungry?" I tried to help out Dina, to get some kind of a response. Besides, we had just spent all afternoon planning a menu and shopping for food with the primary goal of making our parents remember how much they liked each other. We hadn't even started to cook, and it already seemed as though the plan was a flat-out failure.

"Matt, honey, would you and Dina mind leaving us alone for a little while?" My mom looked as though she were holding back tears. Dina's dad was still staring off into space.

"No problem." Dina answered for us both.

We set our grocery bags down on the floor by the refrigerator. Then we literally tiptoed out of the room, as though we were afraid of setting off a land mine.

In the front hall we stopped at the bottom of the stairs. In unison we sat down on the third step. It didn't seem as though there was anything else to do. We listened.

Suddenly the voices in the kitchen got louder. Dina was chewing her nails, a habit that I had noticed appeared only when she was especially tense. I felt like chewing my own. What was going on?

Eventually my mom's voice rose to a pitch that could be heard even from where we sat.

"Then I guess it's decided, Greg. You'll be moving out at the end of the week. Okay?"

"Fine." Dina's dad's voice, equally loud, equally angry, rang out through the heavy door.

Beside me Dina chewed at a nail.

So much for the family dinner.

Later that night Dina locked herself in her bedroom, complaining of a headache. Greg disappeared. My mom went over to her best friend Christina's house. I was again left sitting alone in front of the TV.

I flipped idly from channel to channel.

Why bother? There's never anything good on television.

I sat blindly in front of the set until the phone rang halfway through a *Baywatch* rerun I had already seen.

"Hello?" I answered the phone.

"Matt? Is that you? It's me, Dad." The connection wasn't great. But I was so relieved to hear a sane and happy-sounding voice, I didn't even mention it.

"Boy, am I glad to hear your voice, Dad," I told him.

"How's everything in Boston? Do you miss sunny California yet?" His voice was cheerful. He didn't sound like a guy who had been pining away.

"Boston's fine." I wasn't sure if I wanted to spew out the whole story over the phone. "I mean, there's a lot of stuff going on."

"What do you mean, 'stuff'? Is everything okay?" I decided against the confession. Why involve yet another person?

"Yeah, everything's fine. Great."

"Well, everything is great here too. In fact, I've been dating a woman who's working on this assignment with me. I think you'd like her. She's from L.A."

"That's great, Dad," I heard myself saying. Much to my surprise, I actually did think it was great.

"I've also got some big news I want to discuss with you, as it affects you pretty closely."

"Uh-huh." At this point I was so wary of any and all "big news" that I was instantly on guard.

"I've got a really terrific offer to remain in Singapore for a year and establish this company in the international marketplace. I want to take it.

160

But I won't even consider it unless you tell me you'll think about relocating to the East Coast for your senior year. I want you to be close to your mom if I'm so far away. I don't want you out in California all alone."

"But what about all my friends?" I thought of Andy and Brandon. They would be forced to take in a geeky freshman as their third roommate. All the upperclassmen had been living with each other for years and wouldn't consider a switch.

"And my team?" I had already been elected co-captain for the upcoming season. That would be really hard to give up. And it was impossible to predict whether or not another school would let me on the team as a senior, no matter how good I was. Most coaches preferred to build a team up over time.

"Look, I know it's a lot to think about," Dad said. "And I don't want to put any pressure on you. I would be happy to come back to the States. I've got a lot of work going on at home. But I thought I'd mention it, let you toss the idea around for a while."

I didn't answer right away. I was thinking about what it would be like to live in Boston. Dave's team, Brookline High, Dina.

Dina.

"How's your mom?" My dad hadn't even noticed that I had been spacing out. "Is she still seeing the professor?"

He didn't sound angry or jealous. Just curious. In a friendly sort of way.

"She's good. And yes, Greg's around a lot." Of course at this point I was doubtful that would be true for much longer. But it seemed neither the time nor the place to get into it with my dad.

"Well, send her my best. And give me a call when you've had time to mull this over."

I hung up the phone and picked up the remote again. *Baywatch* had ended, but there had to be some other stupid show I could not watch while I went over my problems in my mind for the hundredth time.

Now I had even more to think about than before. There were all sorts of temptations to moving back in with my mom, but there was a downside too.

For example, everything was so up in the air. My mom and Greg were probably breaking up, thanks to me. And as for Dina, who knew anymore?

Moving to Boston could be great—if somehow a genie would come and wave a wand and everything would be normal again.

It would be horrible if my mom and Greg broke up, leaving my mom lonely and depressed. And what if Dina never forgave me? I would have to see her in the halls every day at my new school.

One thing and one thing only seemed definite. For the first time in years, the first time ever, I understood one vital fact about my family.

My parents are not getting back together. Not now, not ever. The fact didn't even sound so bad.

THIRTEEN

DINA

THE NEXT DAY I was filled with resolve. Before I could lose courage, I jumped in my car and sped to my dad's on-campus office at Boston University.

Summer at Boston University was even busier than the rest of the year. Every student on the East Coast and beyond wanted to take summer classes in Boston. After my tenth circle of the campus a delivery truck pulled out of a parking spot right outside the psychology building.

I had no choice. I simply had to make a full confession to my dad. I had never felt so horrible about anything in my entire life. After my mom had died, my dad had been so good to me. Her death must have been worse for him than I could even imagine. Yet he had been there for me every step of the way. Since the dinner Matt and I had shopped for hadn't worked out, I would have to fix things on my own.

After the funeral my aunts Sherry and Linnea had both offered to take me in for a couple of weeks. They thought my dad needed time to "get himself together." He had refused. "We'll get through this as a family or not at all," he had said.

And what did I do to return all of this selflessness? The very first time he met someone who was actually good for him, I did everything I could to break them up.

All I've ever wanted was for my dad to be happy. I hoped it wasn't too late to tell him so myself, face-to-face.

The psychology building was packed with summer-school students and working professors. Ms. Haworth, who had been the receptionist for years, was sitting at the front desk, knitting a sweater.

She had made one for my birthday once, and I still had it. The sleeves were so long, they reached to my knees. I had worn it anyway.

"Hi, Ms. H." I smiled but glanced at my watch so she would know I was in a rush.

"Hi there. Long time, no see." Ms. Haworth waved a knitting needle at me.

"Is he—" I gestured down the hallway in the general direction of my dad's office. I knew I looked as though I had been crying, but I didn't care. Ms. Haworth was far too sensitive to call me on it.

"He's in, sweetie. But tread lightly. He seems pretty upset."

You're telling me.

I smiled gratefully and walked down the familiar

corridor. *I wonder where Nancy's office is? I've never even asked. That was thoughtful.*

When I got to my dad's door, I stopped walking. The writing on the little nameplate below the window panel was nearly worn off. I made a mental note to have a new one made for him. That was the kind of thing he would never remember. I didn't want all of those Introduction to Psychology students wandering the halls for hours, wondering where spacey Mazlin's office was.

Standing on my toes, I peeked in the window. There he was, sitting slumped over his desk. Every molecule of his seated form said "do not disturb." His head was in his hands. Either he was deep in thought or asleep. I figured it was the former.

I went so far as to put my hand on the doorknob. But I didn't turn it and push open the heavy door. I couldn't make myself do it.

Wiping my sweaty palm on my shorts, I turned and ran back down the hallway.

"Dina, is everything all right?" Ms. Haworth called after me. I was already halfway out the door.

I ran to my car. My hand shook when I put my key in the lock to open the door. Finally I yanked open the door and sank into the bucket seat. I was furious with myself. I had chickened out at the crucial moment. I leaned my head on the steering wheel.

Could I ever right this wrong, or was it just too late? Too late for all of us?

★   ★   ★

"Popcorn."

"Check."

"Diet Coke."

"Check."

"Milk Duds."

"Check."

"Brad Pitt."

"What?"

"Just wanted to make sure you were paying attention." Alison laughed uproariously at her own joke.

"I'm not exactly in the mood, Al." I had only agreed to a film fest because it sounded better than spending my Saturday night home alone thinking about what a mess I had made of my father's life. So far, I wasn't sure I had made the right call.

Alison was in such a good mood, she was nearly giddy. Jason had asked her to go to his parents' house on the Cape for the weekend with his family. And her parents had agreed to let her go.

Great for her, but where did that leave me? Alone and lonely, that's where.

I had finally gotten my best friend back. Now I was about to lose her to some guy. I knew I was being selfish, but I didn't care. Misery loves company, and was I ever miserable.

Not only was I alone, I was also a coward who had wimped out, unable to follow through on important decisions. I had always been so responsible, so mature. What was happening to me?

"What's first?" I asked glumly. I didn't really care what we watched as long as I didn't have to listen to any more ramblings about Jason's perfect ears or darling little collarbone.

"Oh, just a little something I thought you'd like." I knew that tone. She was definitely up to something.

The opening credits rolled. Immediately I recognized the movie. *Sleepless in Seattle*. I had never seen it, even though it had been out on video for ages.

Preparing myself for a misguided movie message on the part of the well-meaning Alison, I settled into the couch and surrounded myself with snacks.

It didn't take me long to figure out what Alison was up to. The movie was about a man and a woman who were meant for each other but almost missed being together due to a twist of fate. Alison was trying to tell me what I had basically already decided. I had to try again to confront my dad. That it was going to be harder than I could even imagine, but that I had no choice. Unless I wanted to tempt fate by keeping two people in love apart.

Apparently she had another message in mind.

"You know," Alison said as soon as the credits started to roll, "Matt really is a great guy."

I tensed up. What did Matt have to do with any of this? We were talking about my dad and Matt's mom, weren't we?

"And he really cares about you," she added quickly. "He told me so."

I sighed deeply. The very subject of Matt had

become a constant source of anxiety. I was beginning to feel like a human yo-yo, up and down, up and down, never getting anywhere.

"I don't know, Al," I said. "I'm beginning to think I'm not cut out for romance in any capacity. First I screw up my own love, then I wreck my dad's. I'd be willing to bet that Matt would rather just forget about my sorry existence at this point. We've been driving each other crazy for too long."

"Is that what your heart tells you?" Alison gave me a knowing look as she chewed contemplatively on Milk Duds. "Or what you think you should be telling yourself?"

"I don't know." I sat on my hands so I wouldn't keep biting my nails. I was beginning to think *Sleepless in Seattle* hadn't been such a hot idea after all.

"Dina. I know you better than that, remember?" Alison wasn't about to let me get away with anything. She never did.

"You're right. My heart tells me that we still have a chance. I just don't know what to do about it."

Alison pointed at my keys. "Whatever you decide, you can't do it from here. Come on, get out of here." She gestured at the front door.

"As usual, you're right." I grinned at her. "I'm out of here," I said, grabbing my keys from the coffee table. Maybe it was too late to repair matters between Nancy and my dad, but it looked as though there was some hope for me and Matt!

FOURTEEN

MATT

GREAT. A TV dinner on the patio. Alonesville. What a way to spend a Saturday night in the height of summer. Weren't these supposed to be the best years of my life? What happened to hot dates and parties and "girls, girls, girls"?

Or at least one five-foot, seven-inch blond girl who happened to be living in my house.

If Andy and Brandon could have seen me now, sitting out here with a Hungry-Man, they would have told me I should have taken the camp counselor job. So far all I had gotten out of Boston was about five hundred mosquito bites and a whole lot of misery.

As I chewed the tasteless turkey breast I could hear my mom on the phone in the house. I wondered who she was talking to. Could it be Greg?

In spite of my better judgment and all I had

learned about dishonesty over the past few weeks, I couldn't help myself. I crept over to the kitchen window. Now I could almost make out what she was saying. But not quite. I tiptoed through the carefully planted herb garden.

At the window I stood just high enough so the top of my head couldn't be seen over the window ledge.

"Mmm–hmm. Yes. I know," I heard Mom say. I could just imagine her cradling the receiver between her chin and her shoulder as she tried to drink a cup of coffee while she talked. She always had to be doing several things at once. Dad used to nag her about it, I remembered. "What if you spill that hot coffee all over yourself?" he'd say. She would just roll her eyes.

Greg had thought she was adorable. I had seen him imitating her, lovingly, and they had both laughed.

But I couldn't glean much from what she was saying. What was going on? I was becoming as gossipy as Alison, but I didn't care. I had to know if my machinations were irrevocable or if there was still hope for my mom at least. Were we both doomed to be forever unlucky in love?

"I understand completely. We were both in the wrong. It was just a foolish misunderstanding. In the grand scheme of things, it means nothing at all." Silence. Daringly I looked over the sill.

Sure enough, the phone dangled at a precarious angle while my mom simultaneously sipped from her Professors Make Better Lovers mug, which had always embarrassed me. She was also doodling on a pad of paper on the counter. She was smiling.

The person on the other end of the phone must have said something because she nodded and murmured assent.

I was transfixed, straining to hear every word. Her body language gave no clues. Unexpectedly she turned and placed the phone back in the wall receiver. With her back to the kitchen window she opened the fridge and took something out.

"Matt, I hope you're not crushing my basil," she said, walking out of the kitchen without uttering another word.

I was so startled, I fell backward onto a patch of something—mint, maybe, from the smell of it. I banged my head on the edge of the rock wall when I landed with a thud.

By the time my mom had brought her leftover salad out to the patio, I had reassumed my position at the table and was innocently finishing off the apple pie square of my frozen dinner.

"I don't know why you eat that garbage," she said, wrinkling up her nose. "I told you there was salad and cold pasta from last night."

"I know. Somehow this fits my mood, though."

We sat in silence for a few minutes. Then my mom leaned over and plucked a mint leaf out of my hair. I could feel myself blushing.

"Anything you want to talk about, Sherlock?"

she asked, crumbling the pungent leaf between her fingers.

"Actually I do have a confession to make, Mom."

She deserved to know the truth. As a boyfriend, I was a miserable failure. As a son, I still had hope. The only way I could fully redeem myself, of course, was to convince Greg of the error of his ways, but that could come later. Now was the time for apologies.

"You know all that stuff I've been telling you about Greg?"

"You mean the negative stories?"

"Yeah. And about Dad?"

"You mean the so-good-you-make-him-sound-like-Gandhi comments?"

"Yeah."

"What about it?" I could smell fresh mint and frozen dinner turkey. The combination was nauseating. But I was already in too deep.

"It was all part of, uh, a plan." There. It was out.

"What kind of a 'plan'?" My mom looked immensely curious. Not angry, which I thought was a good sign. But definitely interested, which wasn't quite so good. I had been hoping she would be too upset to listen closely, therefore missing the extent of the description of my unforgivable behavior. No such luck. She was hanging on every word.

"Let's put it this way. We called it Operation Breakup."

"We?"

"Me and Dina."

"Oh, Matt."

I had never felt so ashamed of myself. My mom sounded so disappointed. I took a surreptitious glance at her. She looked tired. I opened my mouth to speak, but she beat me to it.

"Matt."

"Yes, Mom," I answered sheepishly.

"I've been a mom for a long time now, right?"

"Sure." I wasn't sure what she was getting at, but I was more than willing to go along with whatever she had to say.

"And I'm pretty good at it overall, wouldn't you say?"

"Yes," I answered suspiciously.

Where is all this going anyway?

"I know what you've both been up to, and so does Greg. We weren't born yesterday, in spite of what the two of you may think. And incidentally, the Mafia doesn't really hang out much in Brookline these days. Guido and Tony wouldn't really have come here to break Greg's legs if he didn't pay up his so-called gambling debts."

I winced. We *had* been pretty naive with those crazy stories. I always underestimated parents—mine and everybody else's.

"But Mom?" I had one question I just had to ask.

"Yes?" She still looked tired, but she also looked amused.

"What's going to happen with you and

Greg?"

"I'm not sure. But whatever does happen, rest assured it has nothing to do with Operation Breakup. And when I—when we—figure out what we're going to do, you'll be the first to know. I'm getting tired of all this dishonesty and sneaking around."

Suddenly Greg's funny old car screeched up the street, tore around the corner, and skidded to a stop within inches of the garage door.

"I know he's going right through that door one of these days," my mom mumbled to herself.

I was speechless. I didn't think Greg, or his ancient station wagon, had it in them to make such a grand entrance.

Once he had managed to turn off the engine, Greg practically fell out of the driver's seat. He was carrying something—as he got closer I could see it was an enormous bouquet of flowers. Even with my limited floral knowledge I could tell the arrangement was expensive. I could pick out at least two kinds of roses and a lot of other big, fancy-looking blossoms.

"Hey," I said as he approached. But he didn't even seem to notice I was standing there. He walked right by me without a word.

For some reason Mom and I had both risen to our feet when Greg had pulled up in the driveway. She was standing when he reached her.

"Nancy," he gasped, completely out of breath from what must have been the ride of his life. His shirt was untucked from his khakis. His hair was positively wild. His glasses were askew.

"Nancy," he repeated. Before I knew what had hit me, Greg had thrust the immense flower arrangement in my direction and taken my mother in his arms.

My mom started to cry, but her eyes were shining through her tears. Neither of them seemed to notice that I was still standing there, staring. Only now I was clutching the unwieldy bouquet.

Greg dropped to his knees, taking a little velvet box out of his shirt pocket as he did so. I gaped. My mom was still sobbing and didn't notice for a few seconds that Greg was kneeling in front of her.

"I never thought I'd be saying this again to anyone," he announced. "Nancy, will you look at me, please?"

My mom wiped her eyes with a Kleenex from her pocket. "Greg, what are you doing? Are you crazy?"

"Never been more sane in my life."

I took a step back. This was getting weird. He wasn't really going to . . .

"I love you, and I want you to be my wife. Will you marry me, Nancy?"

Yup. I guess he was. That sounded like a proposal to me. I almost dropped the flowers. This was like something out of one of those soap operas Jessica and her friends had always been watching in her dorm lounge.

Just then another car screeched around the corner, just as fast and just as wildly as Greg's had.

To our collective surprise, it was Dina.

Greg grimaced as she rear-ended his station wagon on her wild turn. He didn't even wait for her to get out of the car before he started to yell.

"Dina, you could have killed yourself, driving like that. Like a maniac! And do you even know how expensive car insurance is these days?" He seemed to have forgotten the previous ten minutes entirely. "And why on earth would you be speeding like that in the first place?"

Dina managed to get out of the car and run into her dad's arms—to everyone's surprise.

"Dad, it's all my fault. I thought of the plan. It was my idea. Alison told me, I mean Mom would have wanted, I mean you deserve to have everything. . . ." Her voice trailed off as she too burst into tears. My mom and I just watched. And listened.

"Dina, I don't understand a word you're saying. Pull yourself together and tell me what you're trying to say."

Dina took a deep breath. For the first time since she had pulled into the driveway, she appeared to notice me and my mom. She shot me a quick look and turned back to her dad.

"We called it Operation Breakup. I didn't want you to replace Mom, and I thought you were trying to replace her with Nancy. Basically we, I mean, *I* lied. To you and to Nancy. And

I've never been more sorry about anything in my entire life."

Dina's dad kissed the top of her head. "I know, sweetheart. We know. It's been really tough on you guys, and we're sorry. But when you pulled up here in such a rush, I had just asked Nancy a very important question. In light of what you've just told me, I think you'll be very interested in her answer."

Dina's mouth dropped wide open. Greg walked over to my mom and knelt down at her feet again.

"Well, what do you say?" he asked. "Should we put these kids out of their misery?"

"Oh, Greg." My mom pulled him to his feet. "Yes, yes, yes. A thousand times yes."

Then as Dina and I stood there watching, they kissed.

Suddenly I became painfully, gloriously aware of Dina's eyes on me. I looked down. I was still holding the enormous bouquet of flowers Greg had bought for my mom. Acting entirely on impulse, I thrust them into Dina's arms.

She took them, sniffed deeply, and tossed them gently onto the ground beside her.

Our parents were so wrapped up in each other, they didn't even notice that Dina and I were closing in on each other.

Stepping over the flowers, she fell into my arms. I didn't hesitate. I bent my head and captured her lips with my own. They were soft and warm . . . and inviting.

Scenes flashed through my mind. Other kisses, other days. There was the top of Mount Blizzard. At the stream on our hike. But this was the best one of them all. I ran my fingers through her silky hair. Her hands were on my back. Suddenly she pulled away just a little bit.

"What? Is this okay?" I was terrified she would say we were rushing things. Ask me to give her some space.

She leaned into me again and whispered in my ear, "I love you, Matt Harbison."

"That goes triple for me," I whispered back. And then we were kissing again.

EPILOGUE

DINA

"WHAT DO YOU think about this one?" Nancy and I were in Christie's Bake Shop, looking through photographs, trying to decide on the perfect wedding cake.

I was incredibly flattered that she was placing her trust in me when it came to all the important decisions. She respected my taste and was making me feel a part of the proceedings. We had spent the entire crisp September morning making wedding plans. Each step was turning out to be more fun than the one before it.

"It's all right, but I think this one is gorgeous." The cake I had chosen was the most natural looking of the available selections. It was decorated with real flowers, arranged in swirls around its four elegant tiers. It was the cake I would pick if I were getting married.

While Nancy considered the cake, I ran over the last month in my mind. It had been a whirlwind. Talk about hurricanes! It was as though Hurricane Marriage had blown into town and stuck around like the second coming of Noah's flood.

Over the past month Nancy and I had been to every bridal shop, bakery, flower store, and caterer in the city, trying to ensure a perfect day for the wedding, which would take place at the end of the month.

We figured we had all been through so much to get to this point that we all deserved it. A dream day. I hadn't decided Nancy was perfect or anything, but she was turning out to be more than okay.

The best moment of all, though, had come the week before. Nancy had taken me to an exclusive boutique downtown to help her select a wedding dress. She didn't want anything too white and froufrouy. But she did want a special, elegant, sophisticated gown.

She had tried on dress after dress. As I sat on a white velvet chair in the waiting area, flipping through an old issue of *Bride* magazine, the saleslady had come out with a pile of dresses over her arm. They were all blue, in shades from palest sky to azure, in silks and taffetas. They all looked beautiful to me.

"She wants off-white or ivory," I told the saleslady. "But thanks for bringing these out anyway."

"Oh, no." The woman smiled at me. "These are for you to try on. She told me so herself." She hung the dresses up on the hook in the dressing room next to Nancy's.

This can't mean what I think it means, can it? I wondered.

"Well?" Nancy's voice floated over the top of the curtain that divided our rooms.

"Well, what?" I didn't want to jump to conclusions and embarrass myself.

"I think my maid of honor would look beautiful in blue."

I pushed open her curtain, beaming. For the first time since I had met her, I gave her a hug.

Dear Mom,

I'm writing you a letter in my diary. I hope you don't think that's weird or morbid—I feel as though somehow you'll understand. Dad and Nancy got married this afternoon. She's a very nice woman, and I think she'll be a good companion for Dad. I feel kind of strange telling you this, but I also feel like I have to—for my sake if not for yours.

I had a talk with Dad before the ceremony. He told me that as long as he lives he will never forget you, that he couldn't even if he wanted to. He said you will be a part of him always. He also said that he feels incredibly lucky to have me because

I am a part of both of you—and that will never change, no matter what happens.

I think I understand now. You loved Dad so much that you would not want him to spend the rest of his life alone. He would have wanted nothing less for you had he been the one to die first. And I'm also realizing that I'm growing up. I won't be here to take care of Dad forever.

As for me, I'm really happy with Matt. We've both definitely come down to earth after our fairy-tale ski trip. But all the caring I felt that week is still there; in fact, it's even stronger because now we know each other. Now we're a part of each other's lives and families.

He's an amazing person, and I think he feels the same way I do about Dad and Nancy. It was maybe even harder for him to give up his dream of his mom and dad's reconciliation, but he's coming to terms with it every day.

And of course it took a lot of explaining to make Dad and Nancy understand our history—everything Matt and I have been through together, like meeting on our ski trip, being separated, then being thrown back together out of the blue. But they realize now how much Matt and I mean to each othcr.

And Mom, you will always be my

mother. Thank you so much for making me the person I am and for choosing Dad. I will always love you, and I hope that I will always make you proud.

I love you,
Dina

"Matt?" I put the bowl of popcorn we had been sharing on the floor.

"Yeah?" He didn't look away from the TV. We were cozily watching a Red Sox game in the den. Our parents had gone out for dinner, so we were the only ones home.

My eyes wandered to the newly framed picture on the wall right above Matt's head. It was from the wedding. Our parents had their arms around each other, and they both looked happier than I'd ever seen them. Beside them Matt and I stood, also looking incredibly happy. I noted for the hundredth time that Matt looked amazing in a tux.

I thought about my other family picture, the one of my mom, Dad, and me in Martha's Vineyard. Surprisingly, it didn't make me feel sad. I could find room in my heart for both families: my first family, and my new one. That's the way my mom would have wanted it. And she was right.

"I've been thinking." I held my breath for a moment. Since the wedding everything had been so perfect. Did I really want to bring up a touchy subject?

"I'm staying, if that's what you're wondering." His gaze never veered. "Nice hit!"

"Did you just say what I think you said, Matt Harbison? You're definitely staying in Boston?" I held one of the couch cushions over his head threateningly.

When had he made this decision? And why hadn't he told me right away? I guess it didn't matter. What mattered was that he would be here! Where he belonged.

"Yup. There's a lot of stuff I like about this town."

"For example?" I wanted to hear it out of his own mouth, even though I knew how he felt about me.

"Well, there's the Red Sox. And I like the Celtics too. And there's Herrell's, and Redbones for ribs. The Arboretum in Jamaica Plain, and my favorite Mexican place on Center Street. Concerts on the Esplanade. I like the snow. And the North End. There's a great café there I've got to take you to sometime. And . . ." I waited. "The girls aren't half bad either."

I hit him with the pillow. But not very hard. I had finally found the boy of my dreams. And he was going to be living right here in Boston.

I didn't want to injure him. At least, not before I got to kiss him . . . a million times.

Do you ever wonder about falling in love? About members of the opposite sex? Do you need a little friendly advice but have no one to turn to? Well, that's where we come in . . . Jenny and Jake. Send us those questions you're dying to ask, and we'll give you the straight scoop on life and love in the nineties.

DEAR JAKE

Q: *I'm sixteen, and I live with my older brother, Rick, who is twenty-five. I'm writing because his girlfriend, Lenni, makes me really uncomfortable. She's always at our apartment, and the more time I spend around her, the less I like her. She hardly ever speaks, and she's always shooting me dirty looks. My brother says she's just shy, but I think she's a snob.*

What I don't get is why he's with her. He's usually so outgoing and lively, but ever since they've been together, they just hang around listening to music all the time. I consider myself a nice and accepting person, but she's never responded to any of my attempts to be friends. I mean, she's not even civil. I hate coming home because I always know she'll be there, hovering. Should I tell my brother how I feel?

KS, New Brunswick, NJ

A: The best thing to do in this situation is to approach your brother from the concerned point of view. Tell him you're worried about him because he doesn't seem to be as happy as he once was. You don't even need to mention Lenni in this conversation. He'll start thinking about whether or not he's as content with his situation as he could be. If he decides he's not, the realization will lead him to wonder why.

At a totally separate time talk to him about the fact that Lenni practically lives at your house. Unless he's blind, he must know you're not friendly with her. If you can talk it out reasonably, you can come to some kind of agreement about the amount of time she spends there.

In the meantime try to ignore her the way she ignores you. Don't let her push you out of your own home.

DEAR JENNY

Q: *My best friend, Melinda, is in major trouble, and I don't know how to help her. Her boyfriend, Nate, is totally messing up her life. He tells her that she's fat and teases her about the way she dresses. It really hurts her feelings, but she never says anything. She gets jealous when he talks to other girls, but when she tells him how she feels, he says she's just being stupid. They keep breaking up and getting back together, and all the craziness is starting to affect her grades. She's also been really quiet lately. She used to be the class clown, and now it seems like she never laughs or even smiles. What can I do to help her?*
RT, St. Louis, MO

A: This is the kind of problem that calls for a nice long talk. Get Melinda alone for a one-on-one and tell her about your concerns. This guy is abusing her. He hasn't hurt her physically, but verbal abuse can be just as damaging. The fact that Melinda has become so totally withdrawn is evidence of that. I've always preferred the direct approach in these situations. Ask her if she's happy. I bet if she really thinks about it, she'll realize what you've already noticed—she hasn't even smiled in a long time.

Point out all her great qualities. Pump the girl up. It's obvious that Nate's insults have killed her self-confidence. Remind her of how happy and self-assured she was before she started dating him. She may defend him at first, but once you plant the seed, she won't be able to avoid thinking about it. Then, if you hear her putting herself down, contradict her. Keep at it until she realizes she's too good for her loser boyfriend. Stick by her no matter what. She's going to need to be strong, and she'll probably need a shoulder to cry on. You've already shown yourself to be a good friend by writing, so I know you're up to the task.

Do you have questions about love? Write to:

Jenny Burgess or Jake Korman
c/o Daniel Weiss Associates
33 West 17th Street
New York, NY 10011